CORPORATE LOVE BIRDS

Love is in the air

SID

ISBN 979-8-89277-246-4

This book is dedicated to
"THE NATURE BEINGS"
who guided me to write this book

Contents

CHAPTER 1

Red Rainbow - Hub of Many Businesses

BLUE HEAVEN is a wonderful country somewhere in the middle of the globe. It boasts many beautiful cities and villages. **Red Rainbow** is one of the most beautiful and richest cities in the country, housing numerous prominent family-run businesses.

Few business companies include Shatbhishak Company, Swarnalekha Company, Windsun Company, and Calbrey, to name a few leading family-run business groups.

Mr. Swaminatham and Mrs. Vishali were husband and wife. They had only one son with the name Mr. Shatabhishak. Mr. Swaminatham has a younger brother, Mr. Suryanatham, who looks like Mr. Swaminatham.

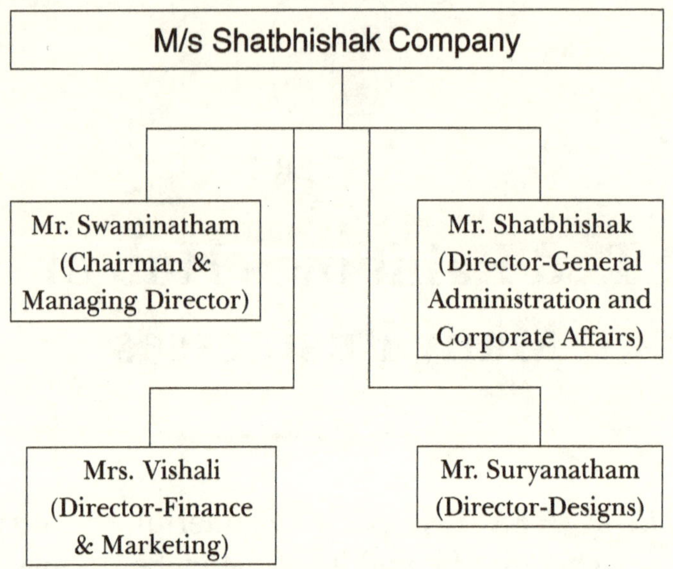

Shatbhishak Company was the leading manufacturer of Vehicles viz cars, luxury buses and similar vehicles.

This company has many branches in other big Countries, Cities and Towns.

Calbrey Company was also involved in the manufacturing of vehicles, viz. cars, luxury buses and similar vehicles. It was the second Top Company after the Shatbhishak Company in the manufacturing of Vehicles.

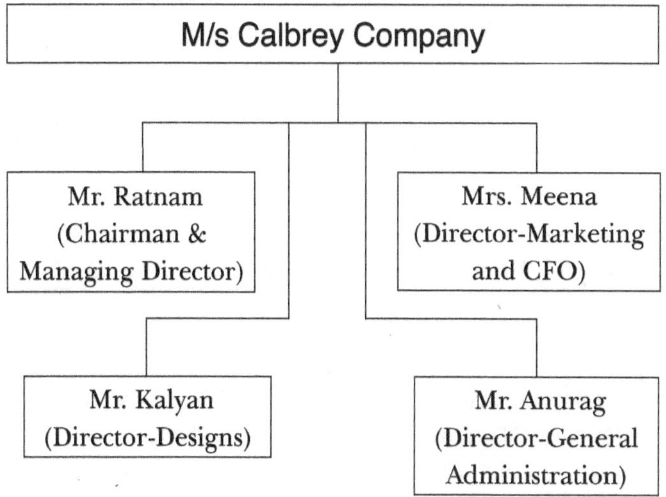

Mr. Ratnam and his Wife, Mrs. Meena, have three sons: Mr. Kalyan, Mr. Anurag and Mr. Vinod. Kalyan was a specialist in designing the models, and he was a great help to his father. Mr. Anurag was not at all interested in the family business. He was fond of horse racing, betting and night parties. Mr. Vinod was working in M/s Shatbhishak Company in the design department as Manager. He was planted there to secretly leak the new designs of M/s Shatbhishak Company with the M/s Calbrey Company. No one in Shatbhishak Company was able to trace him, and it was a top-secret assignment of Vinod.

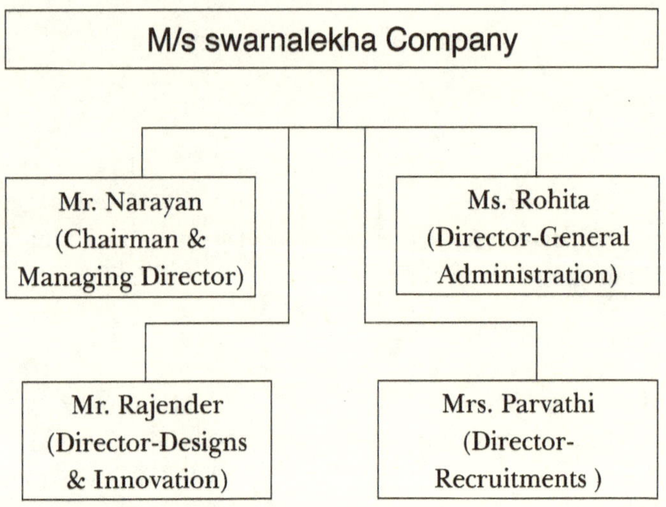

Swarnalekha Company deals in Solar equipment, which is used for street lighting, electricity and various other purposes. Mr. Narayan and his wife, Mrs. Parvathi, had two children, a son, Mr. Rajendar and a daughter, Ms. Rohita. Rohita was not interested in her family business; she had independent views of her life. She wanted to be free from the stressful life.

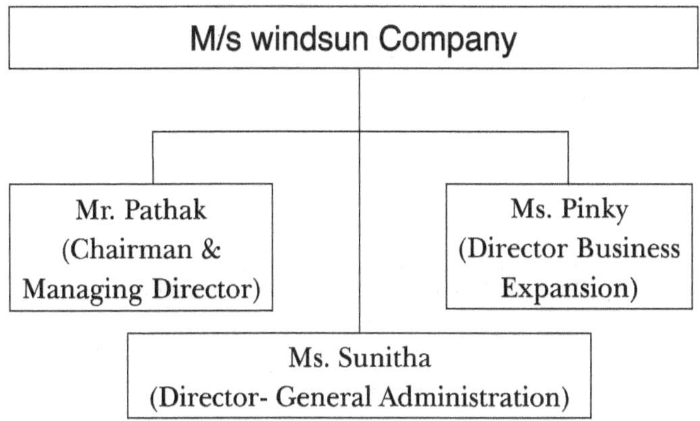

Mr. Pathak had two daughters, Ms. Sunitha (Eldest) and Ms. Pinky (Youngest). His wife passed away in a flight accident. He independently looked after the company and his daughters. Both daughters are of marriage age. Mr. Pathak was eagerly searching for bridegrooms for her daughters.

Windsun Company was a Finance Company that provided finance to various companies. His major shares of finance were given to **M/s Shabhishak Company (50 % finance), M/s Swarnalekha Company (30% finance) and the remaining portion to M/s Calbrey Company (20% finance).**

CHAPTER 2

Arrival of Rohita

Red Rainbow was an important city in the country of **Blue Heaven**. Blue Heaven contained many huge cities such as Baharen, Lakshya, Vimlak, etc. Simultaneously, it contained some villages as well, namely Goutampur, Raygadh, Uttamlanka, and Panchagni.

In the Swarnalekha Company/Family

Rajendar received a message from his younger sister that Rohita was coming from Lakhsya City after completing her modelling sessions. Mr. Narayan (her father) and Ms. Parvathi (mother) were happy to receive her back in Red Rainbow City. They went to the airport along with Rajendar to receive her.

The plane descended from the skies and landed on the ground. Rohita disembarked from the charter flight and approached her family.

She was wearing a yellow t-shirt with blue jeans and black high-heeled sandals, along with a black overcoat. She carried a leather bag in her right hand and a black overcoat in her left. She came closer to her parents and touched their feet.

Her mother, Parvathi, kissed her on the forehead, and their conversation began:

Parvathi: My lovely daughter, Rohita, you are looking so slim. I believe you are avoiding food; now, I will not allow you to go anywhere. I've prepared all your favourite dishes today.

Narayan: We missed you a lot, Rohita. These three years felt very long. I hope your modelling assignments are completed.

Rajender: Father, you must feel happy that after three years, a young and dynamic girl of twenty-four years is coming back alone. I thought she might bring her husband and introduce him to us.

Rohita blushed and decided to tease her brother as she ran behind him, reminiscing about their childhood days.

Narayan: Have you noticed our daughter has grown up, and now we have to find a nice groom for her?

Parvathi: Before searching for a groom, we must ask Rohita if she is in love with someone or wants to get married. Is she ready for marriage?

Narayan: Every girl, before marriage, says she won't marry and leave her parents' house, but she eventually goes to her in-laws' house. This is our family tradition.

Engrossed in these thoughts, they approached their car. In the car, Rajender and Rohita were already seated, waiting for their parents.

Rohita: Have you finished your discussion? I thought my brother and I would have to wait here for two nights until the completion of your discussion.

After that, everyone shared a hearty laugh. They started driving towards their bungalow, cracking jokes and reminiscing about old memories. Once their car reached their bungalow, their servants approached the car to collect Rohita's luggage.

Narayan: Okay, Rohita, you take a good rest. We will have to go to our company, and we'll see you in the evening. *Rajender*: And think about your boyfriend, whom to marry.

Rohita shouted, *"Bro!! I will kill you!! I will settle scores with you once you return in the evening."*

CHAPTER 3

Rohita Decides for Dual Life Adventure

Rohita was neatly dressed, and she was sitting in her room; she was getting bored, so she decided to go to her grandfather's room and see whether she had any material to pass the time. She opened the lock of her grandfather's room and locked herself from inside.

The room was neat and tidy; it contained pictures of scenery and various photos of her grandfather. There was a big almirah which contained some thousands of books. She went near the desk of her grandfather's, and when she opened it, she found a diary of her grandfather. She started reading it. Her grandfather had the habit of writing about his day-to-day work, about the people he met, and about the inner emotions he had on that day. A few glimpses of the dairy were in the below manner.

April 7, 2007

I am feeling frustrated with this life. I want the freedom, the freedom from day-to-day tensions and from the ugly atmosphere.

June 8, 2009

After writing this diary for a long time, I have found a solution to my freedom. I want to live a dual life, one in this city and another in the village. So, I have constructed a secret channel or underground passage with a mini train cabin fitted in that which takes me to the village. And there in the village, there is a haunted old palace where the underground passage doors open, and I can easily go to the village.

I am known as Mr. Vishnu in the city and Ramu in the village. Again, I have constructed a small house in the village for which there is an underground passage that connects to the same train track. The first stop was the haunted old palace where I could go to the outskirts of the village, and the second stop was my house basement. I delegate my work to the junior staff and keep seven days' leave and go to the village, and when I feel like coming back, I say to villagers that I am going to the city to stay at my brother's house and come here in the city by underground passage.No one knows about my dual life until now.

November 27, 2011

I am enjoying my dual life and feeling very happy

March 19, 2012

These may be the last days of my life. I am sick, so I am not able to go to the village but the moments which I have spent there are immemorable.

That was the last time Rohita's grandfather had written, and after that, her grandfather passed away. Rohita was also anxious to lead a 'dual life'; she made a strong decision that she would live a dual life. There was an underground room she checked and found the underground passage fitted with a small train cabin. The machines were in good condition because her grandfather serviced them very regularly. In the meantime, she felt as if someone was calling her from the outside of the room.

*****

She quickly came out of that room and locked it. At night, all the family members were participating, engaging in the following conversation:

Narayan: Daughter Rohita, I think you are free from your ongoing assignments. Now I want you to take part in our company affairs so that we may run the company in a progressive manner.

Rohita: (She was thinking of going to the village and starting another life) aaa... Father, I want to help you, but I have got some important work in Vimlak City. I want to stay there as an unknown person and find out with various leading companies how to run a progressive company, and then I will help you.

Rajender: Oh, that's great! You can see in that city what the leading companies are into and what are the key factors for their success.

Rohita: Okay then, I will be leaving the house tomorrow morning at 9:30 am.

Rajendar: Then I will take you up to the airport.

Rohita: No, brother, I will go my own way; you concentrate on progressing our company. Every minute is very precious to us.

Parvathi: Oh, my daughter! She is so grown up now; she is giving very big suggestions.

In this manner, the night passed. All were thinking that Rohita was going to Vimlak City, but Rohita was preparing herself to go to the village by a secret underground passage.

CHAPTER 4

Rohita Goes to the Goutampur Village

The next morning, Narayan, Parvathi, and Rajendar went to their company together as usual. Rohita was on the way to the market; she purchased some village dresses and quickly came back to her bungalow. Her driver was ready with the car, but she refused and said she would go by cab.

Rohita pretended as if she was going to the airport, but she came behind the bungalow and climbed into her grandfather's room window, which she kept open the other day. She disguised herself as a village girl, took some dresses, and got into the underground room. She sat inside the small cabin and switched the machine. The mini train was on the way to Goutampur Village. This was the same village where her grandfather had stayed as "***Ramu.***"

She was very anxious to go to the village, and within half an hour, she reached the haunted old palace and decided to step down there.

She came out of the old, haunted palace, and she saw how to approach the village. She saw a bullock cart coming towards her. Bullock cart came nearer; the person in that cart was 'Gangaram'. He was the neighbour of Rohita's grandfather, Ramu.

Gangaram enquired: "Hello, young girl, who are you, and what are you doing here?"

Rohita: I am the granddaughter of Ramu, who lived in this village.

Gangaram: What...? You are the granddaughter of Ramu. Then why are you standing there? Come and sit in my cart.

Rohita sat in the cart, and Gangaram took her inside the village.

Gangaram: How is Ramu now? He hadn't visited the village in almost five years.

Rohita: He is no more now. He passed away.

(Gangaram suddenly stopped the cart)

Gangaram: Oh my god!! That's very bad news, he was such a nice helping person for the village. Now, how did you come here then?

Rohita: I came by bus.

Gangaram: Then what are you doing near the old, haunted palace?

Rohita: I didn't know the route so…

Gangaram: Sorry... I didn't ask your name. What is your name, pretty girl?

Rohita: I.. I am Lalitha!

Gangaram: Oh Lalitha!! It's a good name. Your late grandfather and I were very good friends and neighbours. He was a very nice and charming man. But he was very irregular. Sometimes, he used to stay in the village, and sometimes, he went to the city to stay in his brother's house.

See that house (Gangaram showed Rohita/ Lalitha, the house constructed by Ramu, her grandfather) that was constructed by your grandfather. Even now, the house hasn't lost its charm.

Rohita was called as "Lalitha" in the Goutampur village. She entered her grandfather's house. It was kept neat and tidy by Gangaram, and he had one key to that house. Lalitha went and saw the room in the underground of the house and found the secret passage for the small train.

Rohita, aka Lalitha, has now entered the game of dual life living!!

CHAPTER 5

New Ideas Implementation at Shabhishak Company

In Red Rainbow City (Shatbhishak Company), There was a sudden awakening of the office staff members. There was one young man who entered the company wearing a black coat, a charming smile, and a charismatic personality. The staff members greeted him; he was none other than "Shatbhishak", Director of Shatbhishak Company and son of Mr. Swaminatham.

He entered the cabin of Mr. Suryanatham.

Suryanatham: Hello, son, what's up ...

Shatbhishak: Hello, Uncle, what are you doing now?

Suryanatham: I am planning to make a new design for the deluxe coach, but I am not successful yet.

Shatbhishak: I will give you one suggestion that you include in the preparation of the design of your vehicle.

Suryanatham: Okay, Shat, what is it?

Shatbhishak: These days, petrol and diesel rates are skyrocketing, and we need to prepare a model with alternative methods such as solar energy. For this, we need to get associated with a company which deals in solar equipment. M/s Swarnalekha Company is one such company that deals in solar equipment. We should try to get involved with them.

Suryanatham: But who will talk with that company?

Shatbhishak: I will talk with that company's director and Chairman, Mr. Narayan. I also suggest one more idea, uncle. Kindly prepare a model that can help reduce the emission of carbon monoxide into the atmosphere. Please come up with a converter kind of thing which can be fitted to existing vehicles to emit less carbon monoxide into the atmosphere.

Suryanatham: Oh! That's a brilliant suggestion; I will keep this point in front of the board and get approval for the manufacture of the same. You are such a brilliant Shat.

Shat: Thanks, uncle; now I am going to meet Mr. Narayan of Swarnalekha company regarding our plan of Solar-fitted vehicles. By the way, all the best for your new design, uncle.

Surya: Thanks, Shat!

*****

Shatbhishak was in Swarnalekha Company to meet Chairman and Managing Director Mr. Narayan after taking a prior appointment. Mr. Narayan was engaged in a meeting, so he directed his son Rajendar to meet with Shatbhishak.

Rajendar approached Shatbhishak, who was waiting in their conference room, and shook hands with him. They had the following conversation:

Rajendar: Hello Shatbhishak, I am glad to meet you. May I know the reason for your visit?

Shatbhishak: I came here to strike a deal with your company.

Rajendar: What is the deal?

Shatbhishak: I will explain to you that we are manufacturing petrol and diesel engine vehicles, but as you know, the fuels are becoming very scarce. We are planning to manufacture solar-fitted vehicles.

Rajendar: Okay, but how can we help you?

Shatbhishak: You have the major portion in this plan. We need your help to produce solar equipment-fitted vehicles for us. We need to jointly manufacture this by forming a consortium.

Rajendar: Oh wow!! That's a very nice proposal. I really liked it, and let me put this proposal before our board before we can proceed.

Shatbhishak: Okay, Raj, you take sufficient time and don't worry about finance because Windsun Company is providing finance for both companies, i.e. 50% for Shatbhishak Company and 30% for your company, i.e. Swarnalekha Company. When our companies merge, we will have 50%+30% = 80% of finance. That will be sufficient for us to manufacture the Solar equipment-fitted vehicles. Let us quickly make this deal before any other company comes up with a similar idea.

Rajendar confirmed to Shatbhishak that he would convey this deal to their board.

*****

Rajendar met with his father Narayan and briefed him in detail about the meeting with Shatbhishak. Narayan immediately called for a board meeting. Within a short time, all the board members assembled.

Narayan: Dear all, as you all know, our company is facing a bad market, and we are unable to survive due to tough competition. At this time, if our company merges with Shatbhishak, I believe the good time for us will begin.

Parvathi: What is the deal about, sir?

Narayan: Shatbhishak wanted to manufacture solar-fitted equipment vehicles. For this, they wanted us to supply the solar equipment, and when we merge, both company's finances will also be helpful for us.

One of the board members propounded: Sir, it's better we merge with Shatbhishak Company for only 50% because if this new model is not completely successful, then our entire company will not get into the doldrums. We can continue to work with our existing market and our existing clients.

This idea was appreciated by all board members, including Parvathi and Rajendar.

Finally, the Swarnalekha Company decided to merge with Shatbhishak Company for 50% and not the complete merger.

CHAPTER 6

Board Meetings at Shatbhishak and Calbrey

There was a board meeting going on at Shatbhishak.

Swaminatham: Dear gentlemen and ladies, we have given an open offer to Swarnalekha Company to have a joint venture with us to manufacture solar equipment-fitted vehicles. For this, I need your suggestions.

Vishali: I foresee that even though we have given an open merger offer to Swarnalekha Company, they may not merge their company 100%. They may either go for a 50% merger or so, even though they are not doing well in the market.

Another point is we are getting finance only from Windsun Company; if Swarnalekha does not merge with us completely, we will have a shortage of finance, so we need to search for another finance company.

Vinod: Yes, sir, Madam has given the very right suggestion at the right time. I believe we must go for a joint venture with M/s Calbrey Company, which may be a nice deal for us so that our competition may end and we can get good help from them.

Shatbhishak: I already investigated M/s Calbrey; they are the weakest company. They steal the designs of leading companies and release their vehicles with their brand name. Hence, the suggestion of a joint venture with M/s Calbrey is a bad idea; this point was supported by all the board members.

The conclusion of the meeting was:

1. Search for other finance companies which can provide finance for them other than M/s Windsun Company.

2. Search for another company that can merge with them in their existing business.

3. The merger of M/s Shatbhishak and M/s Swarnalekha Company at the percentage which they offer to Shatbhishak.

Vinod was very angry that Shatbhishak had spoken harsh words against his father (Mr. Ratnam) and his Company (Calbrey). He quickly informed his father that M/s Shatbhishak was searching for a joint venture with M/s Swarnalekha Company.

*****

At M/s Calbrey Company, they arranged for a board meeting.

Kalyan: Sir, we know that M/s Shatbhishak Company is our immediate competitor, so we should make a few decisions swiftly to overtake them.

Ratnam: don't worry, we have to take a major step. M/s Shatbhishak Company had decided their failure by rejecting our joint venture. The first and foremost thing we have to do is withdraw the financial support of M/s Windsun Finance Company from M/s Shatbhishak Company and create a dispute between Swarnalekha and Shatbhishak. Another point to be noted is to find out the weakness of M/s Windsun Finance Company and make them support our company in financing us with 100% financing.

The conclusion of the meeting was:

1. To destroy Shatbhishak Company to the gross root level.
2. To create a dispute among Swarnalekha and Shatbhishak Company.
3. To make Windsun Finance Company dance to the tunes of Calbrey Company.

CHAPTER 7

Life at Goutampur Village for Lalitha

It was a nice, pleasant morning for Lalitha (Rohita). She could see the different birds flying in the sky and the different varieties of flowers in her compound. The whole village was very busy, as if they were going somewhere.

Lalitha was well dressed in village girl attire. Gangaram called Lalitha and said:

"Oh, pretty young girl, are you not joining us for the village exhibition? Come with us."

Lalitha came out quickly from her house. Gangaram, his wife **Laxmi,** and his young unmarried daughter **Sukanya** were readily seated in the bullock cart. Lalitha, too, joined them in the bullock cart. While passing through, Lalitha could see the green paddy fields, the cock and hen and their little chickens, duck in the pond swimming with their little ducklings, and there was greenery everywhere.

Lalitha spoke with herself- "This was the atmosphere which I wanted. Finally, I got it. But how can I stay here continuously? I have to go back to Red Rainbow City before my father and mother start investigating about me."

To her surprise, she reached the village exhibition, which was heavily crowded with many villagers. She could find young girls roaming very actively in the exhibition and purchasing bangles, earrings, etc. There was a local wrestling competition, a giant wheel ready for people, etc.

Lalitha and Sukanya spoke about the village and its villagers; they were in different world discussing the exhibition. They both became good friends and went from shop to shop to purchase bangles, earrings, eyeliners, nail polish etc. Gangaram and his wife Laxmi moved towards participation in the '*Spiritual Discourse Session.*'

Sukanya: How do you stay alone in your house (house of your grandfather)? My father was a bit worried about you.

Lalitha: I like staying alone at the house.

Sukanya: you are a very daring girl. I am afraid to stay alone at night.

Lalitha: There is nothing to be scared of at night.

Sukanya: What is your future plan? How many days will you stay here?

Lalitha: Actually, I have to go back to Vimlak City since I have a sister over there. But I will come and go frequently and irregularly. Sometimes, you may also not be able to know when I come and when I go.

Sukanya: What ... I am not able to understand what you are saying.

Lalitha: I will explain this to you later, but first, let us enjoy the exhibition.

People were crowded at each shop's eateries; there was one snake man showing a snake dance, and a few people were enjoying the wrestling, etc. The atmosphere around was very pleasant.

In the meantime, one man came with arrogant body language and a poisonous smile on his face, arguing unnecessarily with villagers, teasing young girls, and scolding everyone around him.

Lalitha asked Sukanya who was that man.

Sukanya: He is ***Birju,*** an arrogant man in the whole village. He teases everyone. He is the son of ***Lampatlal,*** our village sarpanch. Lampatlal is a very rich person in this entire village, so his son Birju's arrogance is because of that.

Lalitha: Gosh! This kind of person is also in this village. I can't believe it.

Then Lalitha and Sukanya moved towards the huge gathering where many people had gathered. There was a wild bull that was tied with rope, and an old man shouted, "Come on, young guys! Come on! Show your strength and fight with this bull by injuring it or controlling it and get the gift in cash or kind."

Sukanya: This is a very cruel game. Every time, a young man enters court to earn money by paying half the price of the gift amount in anticipation of getting the amount doubled after controlling the bull. But he loses his deposit amount, and he gets injured very badly. Until now, there is no strong man who has injured this bull and attained the doubled amount.

Many young men entered the ring to fight with the bull, but they did not succeed. There was one young man who was indecisive to go into the court and fight with the bull. At that time, Birju pushed that man forcibly into the court.

Sukanya: Oh, God!

Lalitha: What happened?

Sukanya: That young man who entered the court is ***Raghu.*** We both have been in love for quite some time. This is not known to our parents or villagers. He was just watching the show, and that cruel Birju pushed him into the court. We have to do something to stop the bull from injuring Raghu.

Lalitha: The ropes of the bull are loosened and it is swiftly approaching Raghu.

Sukanya pleaded with the young men around them to stop the cruel game, but nobody responded; instead, they started yelling more. Sukanya was very sad, and she started crying. At that time, Gangaram and Laxmi completed their spiritual discourse session; they came and stood beside Lalitha and Sukanya. Sukanya controlled her tears so that the villagers and parents didn't get any clue about their love.

So, Lalitha and Sukanya were forced to watch the cruel game in a sad mood. But Birju was enjoying this game very much. Raghu was now fighting with the bull, and everyone in the crowd shouted- "come on! come on!" But soon, the bull injured Raghu very badly.

Now, the bull was going towards Raghu to stab him with its horns. Sukanya started praying to god to show some mercy on Raghu.

Lalitha shouted in her loud voice: "There is no brave young man to stop this situation or at least help that young man from getting injured?"

Then, a young, brave, healthy man who was in village attire wearing a 'Dhoti and Kurta' came on the white horse galloping on it. The villagers got away, giving way to him; he jumped with his horse inside the court, quickly got down his horse, and stopped the bull from approaching Raghu.

Everyone was relieved. One of the villagers shouted, "Here comes the truly brave man, a hero."

Lalitha and Sukanya are also relieved that Raghu is now safe. Villagers brought the injured Raghu out of the court, and they started applying some antidote on him. Sukanya ran towards Raghu to see the whereabouts of him. Lalitha's eyes were glued on the young man who just saved the life of Raghu.

The old man who was the owner of the bull screamed at that brave man- “Hey, you cannot interrupt this game; if you want to enter this game, pay me 500 bucks and get it doubled once you win.”

The brave young man, whose name was ***Suryaa***, said: “Why are you worrying about money? You take my horse; If I win, I will get it from you back or else you keep it.”

Now, the old man took the horse away from the court. Lalitha was still mesmerized and started watching the young man. The bull was cruelly looking at Suryaa and was ready to fight. Gangaram and his wife Laxmi didn’t see Sukanya rushing towards Raghu because they, including most of the villagers, were focused on the bullfight.

The Bullhead and horns were red in colour, and it was very angry, and it marched towards Suryaa instantly. Suryaa stopped the bull with its horns, and a big fight started between them. The cruel Birju was also watching to know who would win this game.

Suryaa jumped on the bull and gave a big blow in its stomach, but still, the bull marched towards him in rage. He then twisted its front legs and injured him. But still, the bull was not ready to accept its defeat. It attacked Surya with its horns, then he held the horns of the bull, rotated it and threw it off forcibly. The bull fled in the air for some time and then fell on the stack of logs, unconscious.

Then Suryaa got hold of the old man who was trying to escape and gave him two blows in the midst of the court and said, "You use this pitiful animal for cruel deeds; come on, give me my horse and money you looted from all youngsters. If you are visible here with that animal once again, then I will tear you apart."

Lalitha jumped with joy, and every villager felt happy, and they lifted Suryaa on their shoulders. Birju was very upset that brave young man Surya took all the attention of the villagers. Now, he wanted to do something to become the center of attraction for all the villagers. He was not very brave to go for bullfights, so he was wondering what to do. Then he saw Lalitha standing alone and watching Suryaa. Then, a cruel idea came to Birju's mind: what if he took Lalitha in the middle of the crowd and slapped her? Then, everyone would draw attention towards him.

He pulled aside Lalitha and grabbed her in the middle of the crowd. Everyone was stunned to see this act of Birju. But they did not respond to his act because he was the son of the rich man in the village. At that time, Suryaa got down from the shoulders of the villagers and went in front of Birju and, gave him a big blow on Birju's face and hit him heavily in his stomach. Birju was a very lean man; he fled in the air for some time, landed on a bangle shop, and fell unconscious.

Lalitha was very impressed with this young man, Suryaa. She suddenly felt something was happening inside her heart, and some butterflies were flying in her stomach. Lalitha asked the young man through her eyes?

Surya replied with his eyes: "For you, I am the thief of your heart, who has stolen it, but for my remembrance to you, let me tell you my name …I am Suryaa."

Then Gangaram and Laxmi approached Lalitha, asked her whereabouts, and thanked Suryaa for what he had done.

Then, all the villagers shouted in chorus. "Suryaa!! Suryaa!!

Then, Suryaa got on his horse, galloped in front of everyone and vanished into thin air.

CHAPTER 8

Lalitha Falls in Love with Suryaa

It was already seven in the evening. Lalitha was in her house and busy thinking about something. Sukanya entered her house and said- "Lalitha, what are you doing?"

Lalitha: Nothing in specific; I was just watching the stars, which were visible from my upper window.

Sukanya: Yes, you can do that activity as well.

Lalitha: Keep aside all these things; tell me, what happened to your future husband, Raghu?

Sukanya: (Shyly) Lalitha, get aside. Still, he is only a lover and not a husband! He is alright now, but there was a huge scream and a lot of hollow bellows, and you shouted at the top voice. What has happened?

Then Lalitha narrated the whole story and bravery of Suryaa.

Sukanya: Which says that the young man is charming, handsome and lovable.

Lalitha: Oh Sukanya! Shut up, and there is nothing like that.

Sukanya: See, Lalitha, I am an experienced holder in lovemaking, so I can make it from your expressions that there is something between you both.

Lalitha: Okay, okay, yes, I felt some attraction from his side. I don't know what it is.

Sukanya: Don't worry. Young man Suryaa is a devotee of Goddess Kali, and we can meet him there. He comes daily in the morning to offer prayers to her.

*****

It was already seven in the morning when Sukanya and Lalitha reached the Kali Temple. Both were waiting for Suryaa. As the sun rose from the mountains and birds started chirping, a young man came galloping on a white horse; he was Suryaa.

Sukanya: Hey Lalitha! Watch from here. We can see him. Now, I don't have any role here. I have to meet Raghu. Call me once you are ready to return to the house.

Suryaa came nearer to the temple and went inside. He offered prayers to Goddess Kali, and while returning, he saw Lalitha was engrossed in prayer.

Suryaa: Did you sleep well last night?

Lalitha: I am Lalitha. I didn't get any sleep last night.

Suryaa: Okay, then come with me.

He then took her towards the paddy green fields, and there he stopped his horse under a nice shadow of the tree. They then exchanged their inner feelings with each other.

The days passed, and two months had already passed. Sukanya and Raghu, Lalitha and Suryaa were regularly meeting at the paddy field in the morning and evenings.

Lalitha remembered her time to go back to her city. She met with Suryaa and told him she had to go to Vimlak City to meet her sister and she would be back very soon. She told Suryaa to wait for her near the old, haunted palace, and after one month, she could be seen there. She also conveyed the message to Sukanya, Gangaram and Laxmi that she would be back in a month.

The next day, she left the place under the secret train and quickly arrived at Red Rainbow City. Lalitha wanted to keep the secret of her dual life a secret, so she did not reveal it, even with Suryaa.

*****

In a short time, Lalitha, now Rohita, reached the basement of her grandfather's room. It was already night, and she slowly opened the window of her grandfather's room, slid down, jumped the compound wall of her bungalow, and booked a taxi for the airport.

Now she called her father Narayan to pick her up from the airport. It was already 3:30 am in the morning. Rajender came to pick her up from the airport.

Rajendar: So my sister, how was Vimlak City and how was your experience in learning new strategies from various companies?

Rohita: It was a very nice trip, brother, and I enjoyed working with nice guys. Now, what is the position of our company?

Rajendar: Our company has merged 50% of our shares with Shatbhishak Company, and tomorrow, both families are throwing a big party for our clients, shareholders, and directors. You have just arrived at the right time.

*****

It was a nice evening for two business families. Shatbhishak Company and Swarnalekha Company. Everyone was enjoying the music, the delicacies, the dance and the drinks.

Shatbhishak: Vinod, we have invited all the business families of our city, and I didn't see anyone coming from Calbray Company.

Vinod: I think they are very busy, sir.

Shatbhishak: Nonsense! At least they should send someone from their company to attend on behalf of their top management.

All of a sudden, a car stopped, and one young lady stepped out of the car; all eyes were on her.

She was Rohita. Shatbhishak saw her for the first time and felt she was his first love!!

Mr. Narayan introduced Swaminatham, Vishali and Suryanatham to her daughter Rohita.

When Rohita met with Shatbhishak, she was shocked to notice that Shatbhishak looked like Suryaa, whom she had met in Goutampur Village.

She pulled Shatbhishak aside and asked hurriedly: "Are you Suryaa?"

Shatbhishak: Young lady, you might have mistaken me for Suryaa, but I am Shatbhishak.

Shatbhishak and Rohita were left alone to talk with each other.

Rohita: Do you have any twin brothers?

Shatbhishak: No, but why are you asking that question?

Rohita: It seems I have seen him.

Shatbhishak: What!! Are you serious?

Rohita was hesitant to reveal the secret, so she pretended as if she was cracking a joke.

Shatbhishak: Then what have you found in my personality?

Rohita: Everything that a successful person needs to have.

Shatabhishak: Okay, then let's make a deal to meet at Clip Knot restaurant tomorrow evening at 8:30 pm.

Rohita: But...

Shatbhishak: No ifs and buts. You have to come for sure. I will wait for you there.

The party was very good, and Rohita felt as if she met with Suryaa.

*****

Days passed, and Swarnalekha Company and Shatbhishak Company started making new models of cars fitted with solar equipment.

Rohita, aka Lalitha, was enjoying her dual life. Shatbhishak was secretly in love with Rohita, but she was in love with Suryaa.

CHAPTER 9

Shatbhishak Meets His Friend Srikanth

Shatbhishak was very busy in a meeting when he got a ring in his extension that someone wanted to talk with him.

When Shatbhishak spoke with that person, he was none other than his longtime friend ***"Srikanth."***

Shatbhishak: Hey Srikanth! It's been a very long time. When did you return from Baharein?

Srikanth: I returned just two days back, and I could not get an appointment to meet you at your office.

Shatbhishak: Yes, friend, we recently had a joint venture with Swarnalekha Company for a 50% share. I was very busy in that aspect. What about you, what are you doing these days?

Srikanth: I worked in a few leading companies to gain experience, and now I am back in my original city after six years. I wanted to do something here.

Shatbhishak: Hey, then, why don't you work for us as 'Head of Marketing & Strategies' and appoint your own team and market our products?

Srikanth: Okay, but what will be my work?

Shabhishak: Your work will include searching for new resources for Shatbhishak company, looking for a new financing arm or company, etc.

Srikanth: Okay, Shat, that's a nice idea. I will start your work from tomorrow onwards. Send me an appointment letter.

Shatbhishak: Okay, I will send it. But how far has your love story gone with '***Shirormani?***'

Srikanth: Still, it is going on. Still, I haven't expressed my inner heart feeling with her.

Shatbhishak: Don't worry, tomorrow is ***the Raakhi Festival***. Every year, both sisters, Shirormani and Shikha, come to our bungalow to tie Rakhi. In return, I bless them as a brother exchange sweets, and we have a lot of gala time.

Srikanth: Wow! That's a nice idea to know what's there inside the heart of Shirormani.

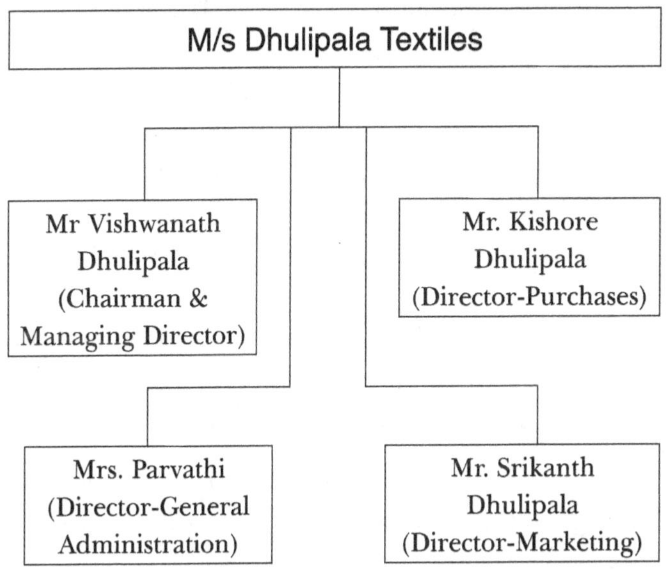

Mr. Vishwanath Dhulipala has a wife named Mrs. Parvathi and has two sons, Srikanth Dhulipala (Elder Son) and Mr. Kishore Dhulipala (Younger Son). They have Dhulipala Textiles

Company, which is the leading garment company in the entire Red Rainbow City.

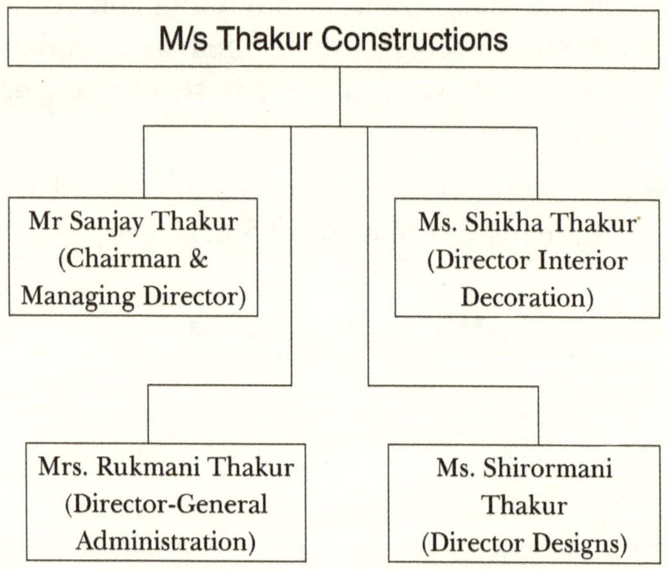

Mr. Sanjay Thakur and Mrs. Rukmani Thakur had two daughters, Ms. Shirormani Thakur (Elder) and Ms. Shikha Thakur (Youngest). They were involved in the construction of bungalows, Villas and Flats. They were one of the leading constructors in Red Rainbow City.

*****

At Shabhishak Company, in Swaminatham's Cabin:

Swaminatham, Vishali, Viswanatham Dhulipala and Parvathi Dhulipala were assembled.

Swaminatham: It's nice to see you after a long time, Viswanath. How is Srikanth and Kishore?

Viswanatham: Well, they all are fine. Srikanth had just returned from Bahrain City two days back, and now he is well-trained to take up new projects. Kishore is somewhat lethargic, but I believe he will pick up quickly at work.

The actual reason why I reached out to you is that I have a huge excess money from my Textile Business; I just wanted your suggestion on where to invest it so that I can avoid keeping the money idle.

Swaminatham: Okay, in fact, our company has only one finance company, Windsun, and that is not giving us 100% finance to our company. Now, we have merged with Swarnalekha Company for 50%. We are in dire need of finance. Why don't you invest your excess funds in our new project and become its financier?

Viswanath: That's a nice idea; I will provide finance to your company and its new projects.

In the meantime, Shatbhishak and Suryanatham also entered the cabin.

Shatbhishak and *Suryanatham*: Hello, Everyone!!

Vishali: Come on, you both have come at the right time. Give us your suggestions in our talk.

Shatbhishak: What decisions you have taken are very nice. Vishwanathan uncle is providing finance to us, and his son Srikanth has been appointed as the 'Head of Marketing and Strategies.'

All said it together: "Wow! That is great news!"

CHAPTER 10

Dharmasena Comes Out of Jail

In the outskirts of Vimlak City

The huge prison doors were opened, and one man came out of the prison. He was "***Dharmasena***"; he had spent one year in prison for robbery in Vimalak City, and after one year, he was set free from prison.

Dharmasena directly went into the 'Uttam Lanka Village', where he had a sister by the name ***"Manasa."*** He directly knocked on the doors of his house, but the doors were locked. In the distance, "***Pappu***" saw Dharmasena looking at the door; he hurriedly came near Dharmasena.

"Hey Dharmasena, you have returned from prison. I am very happy to see you."

Dharmasena also wished Pappu.

Pappu was the childhood friend of Dharmasena.

Dharmasena: Hey, where is my sister Manasa?

Pappu: Dharma, Manasa had gone to Red Rainbow City to become a model.

Dharmasena: (angrily) You didn't stop her.

Pappu: She didn't listen to me; she said she was quite upset with you and your behaviour, and so she hurriedly left for the city. She wanted to settle down as a model there.

Dharmasena: Oh no! Red Rainbow is a big city, and I don't know where she could be. How will I search for her?

Pappu: Dharma, don't worry. I have a nice plan for earning billions of money, lavishness and prestige.

Dharmasena: What is the plan?

Pappu: Look at this newspaper in which a photo of Mr. Shatbhishak is printed for going for a joint venture with Swanalekha Company. He gave an interview in the newspaper about his company-Shatbhishak. He is the son of Swaminatham and the co-owner of the company.

Dharmasena: Hey, his face resembles my face.

Pappu: No mere resemblance, but you are a true photocopy of his face; if we anyway enter into Shatbhishak Company, we may become the co-owner, and we will capture that person, and you will take his place.

Dharmasena: Then I will become rich and find out my sister and show her that I am also a rich man.

*****

Rakhi Festival Celebration

At last, the day had come to enjoy the Rakhi Festival. Every part of the country tied Rakhis to their brothers and received gifts and blessings from their brothers.

Shatbhishak was eagerly waiting for her sister to come and tie Rakhi on his wrist. Then, a car stopping sound was heard in the portico of Shatbhishak's bungalow. Two sisters, Shirormani and Shika, got out of the car and went inside the bungalow.

Shatbhishak received them gleefully, and they had a friendly chat. Then, both of them tied Rakhi on his wrist. Shatbhishak blessed them and gave them gifts on the occasion.

Shatbhishak: You, both sisters, visit only on the occasion of the Rakhi Festival. On other days, you don't even call me; this is not fair.

Shiroramani: Oh brother, I was busy with one leadership conference preparation; finally, it got completed. I am totally free now.

Shatbhishak: Don't worry, I will keep you busy again. You know my friend Srikanth, I appointed him as Head of Marketing and Strategy, and since you are free, you can now join his team and work for my company.

Shikha: Oh great! That's a nice idea.

Shatbhishak: What do you feel, Shirormani?

Shirormani: Yes, that's good. What will my post and work be? Can you be brief?

Shatbhishak: Srikanth will brief you about the work. You will be in the Marketing Team.

Shirormani: Oh gosh! I forgot that my friend is coming to the airport. I need to pick her up. Shikha, you carry on, I need to go.

Shikha: Bro, you are a genius.

Shatbhishak: Why do you think so?

Shikha: You are asking this question with me? Okay, I know that Srikanth is in love with Shirormani.

Shirormani: What! Do you already know?

Shikha: I also know that Shirormani is not interested in him, but the proposal you had kept before her to work with Srikanth is a very nice one. If Srikanth has talent, he will win her heart, and he may make her fall in love with him. So, that was about my sister Shiru, but I have a problem.

Shatbhishak: What's that?

Shikha: I am in love with Ajay Singhal of Singhal family.

Shatbhishak: What are you? You are younger than your sister, but in the matter of love, you are ahead of your elder sister. Then, what's the problem?

Shikha: The problem is I have no way to contact him or spend time with him, so how can I express my love for him? It's only one-sided love from my side.

Shatbhishak: Don't worry. I will manage all that, but you have to help me succeed in my love. Actually, I, too, have fallen in love with Rohita of Swarnalekha Company, and you have to approach her for me.

Shikha: Oh yes! I understand you have given my elder sister the post in Marketing, and now you are giving me the job of a mediator.

Shatbhishak: (Laughing aloud) You naughty girl!!

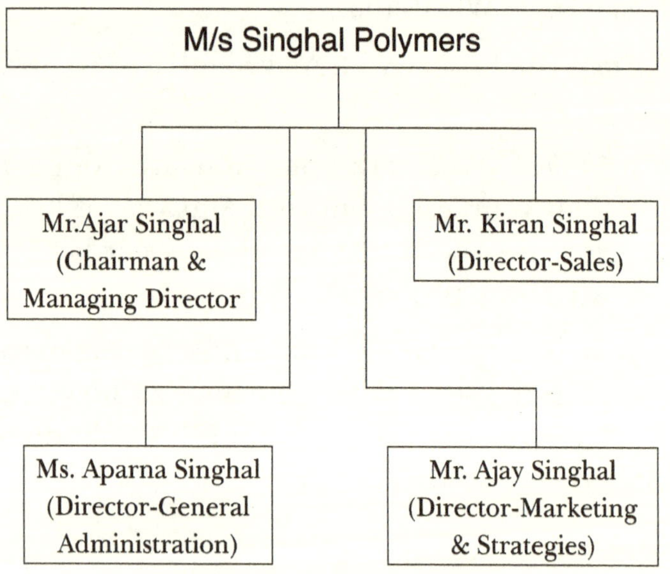

Singhal Polymers was the leading Polymers Company in Red Rainbow City. Mr. Ajar Singhal was the Chairman and Managing Director of the Company. Ms. Aparna Singhal was his wife, and his sons were Mr. Ajay Singhal (Elder) and Mr. Kiran Singhal (younger).

Ajay, Srikanth, and Shatbhishak were classmates, so with that confidence, Shatbhishak told Shikḥa that he would get Ajay and Shikha together.

CHAPTER 11

Calbrey Company Makes a Deal with Windsun Company

In Windsun Company:

Mr. Ratnam had gone to Windsun Company to talk about a crucial decision. He finally met with Mr. Pathak of Windsun Company, the Chairman and Managing Director.

Pathak: It was a sudden and surprise visit by you, sir. Tell me, sir, how can I help you?
Ratnam: Today, I came here not as a businessman but to talk about personal matters.
Pathak: Oh, is it? Please elucidate.

Ratnam: I am in search of brides for my two sons, Kalyan and Anurag, and I have come here to ask both of your daughters to become my daughter-in-law.

Pathak: Oh nice!! That's very good. I was eager to get my daughters married to one decent family. I will not find any more decent family than yours.

Ratnam: So, I believe you have agreed to the marriage of your daughters with my sons?

Pathak: of course, Ratnam ji

Ratnam: I already fixed the date for engagement and marriage by consulting my family's holy priest. Within a week, we will have the engagement; after that, after two weeks, we will organise the marriage. So, you prepare and make arrangements for engagement and marriage.

*****

Finally, the day arrived when both the pairs - Kalyan and Pinky and Anurag and Sunitha- were getting married. All the eminent personalities of Red Rainbow were invited to the wedding ceremony except Shatbhishak and Swarnalekha Company.

Mr. Pathak was very happy that both his daughters were getting married. He was a very proud father. At that time, Mr. Ratnam took Mr. Pathak to one private room.

Ratnam: Mr. Pathak, until now, you were providing 50% of finance to Shatbhishak Company and 30% of finance to Swanalekha Company, and you were giving me a mere 20% of finance. But from now on, you will provide me with the entire 100% finance.

Mr. Pathak was in shock after listening to Mr. Ratnam's words.

Pathak: What are you telling Mr. Ratnam? How can this be possible? No, I cannot do that.

Ratnam: If you don't do that, then I will stop this marriage right now, and your daughters will remain unmarried and have to carry the blame for breaking the marriage for the rest of their lives.

Mr. Pathak was helpless at that moment, so he signed the papers presented by Mr. Ratnam declaring that he would provide 100% of the finance to Mr. Ratnam's Calbrey Company.

CHAPTER 12

Sukanya Gets Married to Raghu

In Goutampur Village

Rohita, aka Lalitha, came to Goutampur village by underground train and met Suryaa regularly. On the other side, Sukanya and Raghu were carrying their love safely.

One day, Birju was passing through the paddy fields in the early morning, and he spotted Raghu and Sukanya making love in the paddy fields. He quickly spread the news about their affair to the entire village.

Gangaram and his wife were very ashamed to stand in front of the Village Committee to discuss their daughter's affair with Raghu. On that occasion, Lalitha was not available in the village. Raghu's father, Kansiram, and Sukanya's father, Ganagaram, were of different castes, and people from different castes were not allowed to get married.

Cruel Birju was very happy that he had made a big problem for Sukanya and Raghu. The Village Committee was assembled to resolve this problem. His father, Lampatlal, was also present in the committee as he was it's head (Sarpanch).

Every villager was accusing the love affair of Raghu and Sukanya. Then Birju told everyone in a loud voice: "Since Sukanya and Raghu had made a big mistake, they should be beaten daily for one hour every day so that they will be aware of their mistake."

Every villager supported this view of Birju, and the Village Committee was about to declare its decision. At that time, they heard the galloping sound of the horse, and Suryaa stepped down from his horse in front of everybody. Birju was afraid to face Suryaa; he hid behind his father.

Suryaa then propounded loudly: "Our Brothers and Sisters, Raghu and Sukanya, were in love with each other; they wanted to get married soon. They have not done anything wrong. They were about to tell their families about this before they were spotted by Birju. In love, there should not be any wall of religion, region, caste, or creed. Love is a precious thing and a divine act of good.

Today, if we stop them from getting married, then there will be no true love, no true lovers, and this world will diminish without love."

He continued- "You were talking about punishment; what crime had they done? Did they kill someone or steal something precious from a rich house? They only loved each other, but in my opinion, it's not a crime at all. The actual punishment should be given to Birju for misbehaving improperly with the women in the village. You all have no guts to stop him or complain about him, but you assembled here to detach the two true lovers?"

Everyone became silent, and Lampatlal was also cautious; he came to know that if he stopped this marriage, then all villagers would complain about his son's bad deeds with them.

The entire Village Committee finally agreed to the marriage of Sukanya and Raghu. Both Raghu and Sukanya thanked Suryaa for supporting them and getting them married.

In a few days, Raghu and Sukanya got married, and there was a true triumph of love!!

CHAPTER 13

New Financer for Shatbhishak

Srikanth was just thinking of the phone call that Shatbhishak had made to him, telling him that he was giving him a great surprise. At that time, somebody knocked on the door, and a sweet voice said, "Shall I come in?"

Srikanth: Yes, come in, please.

To his surprise, Srikanth saw Shirormani standing in front of him; he didn't know how to act at that time; his dream girl and love was before him.

Shirormani: This is my joining report. I am appointed as the ***"Deputy- Marketing Head & Strategies."***

Srikanth: Oh..I see. Please be seated.

Shirormani: Can I know my KPA or Key Performing Areas?

Srikanth: My assistant will explain everything about your work.

Shirormani: Why not you?

Srikanth: Why not me? Because you are interested in starting work at this moment, we have a very crucial decision to take.

Shirormani: What's that?

Srikanth: Before joining here, you might have read the present condition of our company Shatbhishak. It merged 50% with Swarnalekha Company, so our company needs more capital to carry out our new projects. I contacted Mr. Kuber (Chairman and Managing Director of Kuber Financing Company). He has a huge capital to invest, and he has offered it to many leading companies. So we must leave for Vimlak City now that I have booked the flight, and we must take at least 50% financial support from his company. We must hurry up before the Calbrey people approach him, and we must take his big grand support.

*****

At Calbrey Company

Ratnam, Meena, Kalyan and Vinod were in a confidential meeting.

Ratnam: Poor Shatbhishak people, I am getting pity on them. I have grabbed their finance-giving arm. I have a great plan now.

Meena: What is that, my great husband, sir?

Ratnam: You might be knowing the Singhal Polymers in which Mr. Ajar Singhal is a very good businessman. He is a leading polymer manufacturer, and he is the number one leading company in Red Rainbow City. According to my news, he is trying to establish a few industries in other cities as well. I assured him that I would provide finance to him because the Windsun financing company has been captivated by me, and Mr. Pathak did what I said to him.

I also offered his son to work with us as Marketing Head & Strategies to take our relationship to the next level.

Kalyan: Dad, you have taken this big decision without our concern.

Ratnam: Don't worry, my son. This is only a trick to Capture Singhal Polymers. Since we are providing finance and we have appointed his son in our company, he has full confidence in me. So, I will utilise his confidence and grab his company as I grabbed Windsun Finance Company.

Meena & Vinod: Nice. Very nice idea!!

Kalyan: Okay, Dad, then, since Kuber Financing Company has offered us to take finance from them, Ajay Singhal and I will go and talk with them before Shatbhishak representatives reach them.

At Vimlak City

In Kuber Financing Company, many company representatives were present to get the finance for their respective companies. Suddenly, when Srikanth and Shirormani entered the conference hall, everybody was silent, and many company opponents even left that place thinking that they would not get any finance from Kuber Financing Company because Shatbhishak Company was the leading manufacturer of vehicles in the entire Blue Heaven Country.

Soon Ajay and Kalyan too reached there representing their company "Calbrey ". As Ajay,

Srikanth, and Shtabhishak were classmates, Srikanth approached Ajay and exchanged greetings with each other. Srikanth introduced Shirormani to Ajay, and Ajay introduced Kalyan to both of them. Kalyan was the odd man out of the group. He was not able to understand how to react.

Ajay said he was working in the Calbrey as "Head of Marketing & Strategies". Srikanth also told him that he too was working with Shatbhishak as "Head of Marketing and Strategies." Srikanth and Ajay moved to the other part of the hall to have a small private chat.

Srikanth: You have your own polymer company, so why are you working for Calbrey?

Ajay: My father was having some future deals with the Calbrey, which he has not revealed to me yet. For that reason, he has told me to join the Calbrey to have a good alliance.

Ajay: Keep all these things aside; who is that pretty lady with you?

Srikanth: My future wife. I am in the process of making my dream come true, and Shatbhishak is helping me do this.

Ajay: Shatbhishak is the master planner in all kinds of things like this; you know, in college days, he also brought a lot of lovers together and got them married. All the best for your marriage in advance.

Meanwhile, in the Kuber Financing Company, the board meeting was called off, and the members supported giving 60% finance to Shatbhishak, 20% to Calbrey and 20% to the remaining Companies in Vimlak City.

CHAPTER 14

Big Changes and Decisions at Shatbhishak Company

An Emergency board meeting was called out in Shatbhishak Company. Key persons from Swanalekha Company and Dhulipala Textiles were there as well.

Mr. Suryanatham started the meeting with his opening words:

Welcome to all gentlemen and ladies. We assembled today to make huge decisions regarding our Company. Coming to the first matter, i.e. financing, as you all know, previously, Windsun Financing Company was providing 50% finance to Shatbhishak Company and 30% finance to Swarnalekha Company, but they stopped giving us finance abruptly. Now, it is providing 100% finance to Calbrey Company.

But we must be happy that we are getting finance in two ways, one from my friend's Company- ***Dhulipala Textiles*** and another from ***M/s Kuber Financing Company***. So I have decided to restructure our company and go into expansion mode.

Our Present Shatbhishak Company will have the following structure:

The current structure of Shatbhishak Company will be as follows:

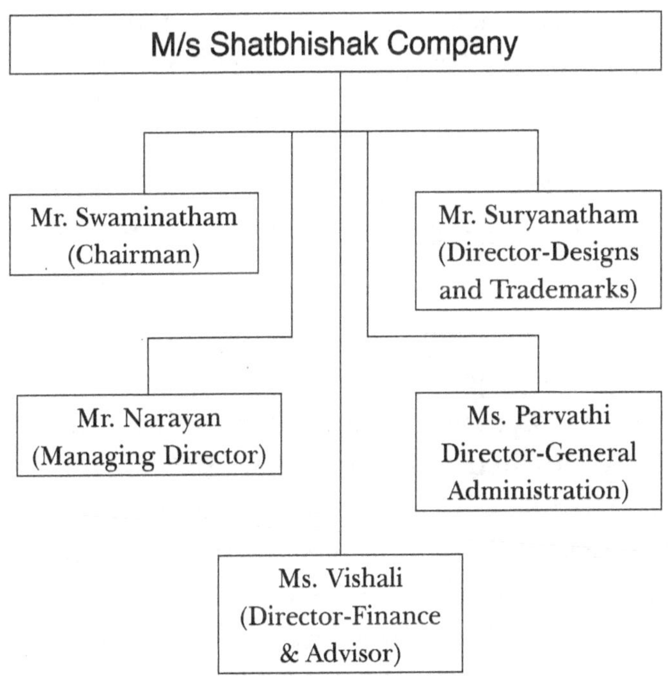

We are planning to start our new venture and its structure and persons will be as below:

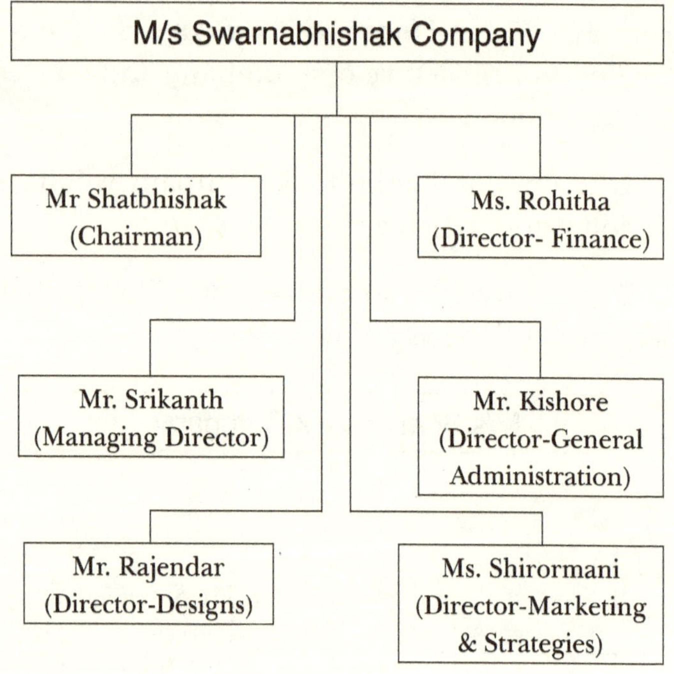

He continued that Shatbhishak Company will get finance from Dhulipala Textiles, and Kuber Financing finance will be utilised for the newly formed company ***"SWARNABHISHAK COMPANY"***. The speciality of this company is it includes all the young businessmen and women from our families!! We are completely dissolving the ***Swanalekha Company***, and its manpower and resources will be utilised for Shatbhishak Company or Swarnabhishak.

This new company, ***SWARNABHISHAK***, will manufacture new solar equipment-fitted vehicles. We will expand our operations in other cities as well for both companies, in Vimlak, Baharein and Lakshya City.

Everybody was happy and felt fulfilled by this decision, and all the members present in the meeting clapped at this decision. Finally, the board meeting ended, and this meeting was the most important meeting in the history of the Shatbhishak Company

CHAPTER 15

Wedding Bells in Calbrey Family

In Calbrey Bungalow

Kalyan got married to Pinky, and they were very happy with their marriage. Pinky quickly gelled with the family, and she was helping her husband, Kalyan, in the business as well.

The marriage between Anurag and Sunitha was a compromise. Anurag, who was Ratnam's second son, was not at all interested in his family business. He was a spendthrift, spending part of his family money on late-night parties, gambling, and horse racing, and he was a drunkard. He didn't even care for his wife, Sunitha; he would give more preference to his girlfriends.

One night, Sunitha was waiting for her husband, Anurag; it was already 2:30 in the early morning. Anurag came to his bungalow; he was fully drunk, and he was not able to stand properly. Sunitha supported him, assisted him to their room, and made him sleep on the bed.

That night, Mr. Ratnam was awake, not as the Chairman of Calbrey but as the father of his son Anurag. He saw tears coming out of Sunitha's eyes. He went closer to her and consoled her by telling her the following words:

"Oh, my daughter! Don't cry. Even though the marriage between my two sons and your two sisters was a selfish business deal, the step also has a hidden reason. Today, I have three sons, Kalyan, Anurag, and Vinod, but I have only two sons, Kalyan and Vinod. I cannot treat Anurag as my helping hand and a son because he cannot help himself, and what help can I expect from him?

I have seen in you the traditional features of a good housewife and a good daughter-in-law, so I know that you are the only one who can take care of my son, correct him, and put him on the right path. I also know that you are the correct partner for him."

After saying these words, Ratnam also wept. Even though any man who looks reserved and serious from the outside (face-wise) is actually smooth and sensitive from the inside (in the heart). Even though the person who looks like a healthy person with a lot of cruelty in him has a sensitive and smooth heart which tells him what is right and what is wrong.

It's not money but a healthy family and healthy family atmosphere that makes the man happy, and if he lacks in his family, he starts searching for that happiness in the outside family or outside world. These are a few naked truths of life!!

*****

In Red Rainbow City

It was Rakhee Festival, and two wrists were ready to get the Rakhi tied on their wrist. The two wrists were of ***Mayank*** and ***Vinay***. Mayank was the owner of the vehicles workshop- "**ALWAYS OPEN**". Vinay was an unemployed youth who came from Bahrain City, but he had no way to get a job, so for the time being, he started working with Manyank in his workshop. Mayank and Vinay became good friends in a short time. Mayank had a younger sister by the name "***Sharada***". Sharada also treated Vinay as her brother.

Sharada tied Rakhee to Vinay and Mayank, and both gave her surprise gifts wrapped in a colour wrapper. After that, Sharada left for her traditional dance class. Mayank and Sharada's parents died at a very young age, and they were parentless at that time. They were supported by ***James D'Souza,*** who was the then-owner of Car Workshop-**ALWAYS OPEN**. After his death, Mayank took over as the owner of the same Car Workshop. Both of them lived in a small house which was built at the backside of the car garage.

Mayank and Vinay got busy repairing the cars.

Suddenly, a luxurious car with two flat tyres entered their garage. Srikanth and Shirormani came out of the car. Mayank went nearer to Srikanth and said: "You are Srikanth, right? You are the new managing director of Swarnabhishak Company; the news was all over the newspaper and media."

Srikanth: Yes.

Mayank offered them coffee and treated them as guests. Mayank introduced his friend Vinay and asked for a job offer in his company. Vinay was highly competent, and after seeing his educational certificates, he offered him in the accounts department as a Junior Officer (accounts). he assured them that if his work was found satisfactory, then a promotion and salary hike would also be given.

In exchange, Vinay also briefed Srikanth about Mayank's good knowledge of car repair and design. Srikanth felt that Mayank would be of great help to them in the new car design on the production side. So he offered a job to Mayank as well.

*****

On the other side of the city, Dharmasena and Pappu had reached the Red Rainbow City in search of their sister Manasa. They were very unhappy that they were away from her on the day of the Rakhi Festival.

CHAPTER 16

Vinay's Real Family Details Were Hidden

Shabhishak stopped his car in front of the old, haunted house on the outskirts of Red Rainbow City, and he got out of the car. He got a call from an unknown person stating that he would reveal some of his company's hidden secrets and directed him to reach a haunted house located on the outskirts of the city.

Shatbhishak stepped inside the house, and somebody wanted to hit him hard on his head, but he rescued, and he gave a big blow to that person.

*****

Manasa (Sister of Dharmasena) was searching for an institution which could train her in modelling. While in the process, she met with ***Suchitra***, who was working as a model in Red Rainbow City. Suchitra escaped from her house to become a model. Actually, Suchitra was the daughter of ***Shammi Kuber***- Chairman and Managing Director of **Kuber Financing Company**.

Vinay worked in the garage, "Always Open." He was the elder brother of Suchitra and the Elder, son of Mr. Shammi Kuber and Ms. Mohini Kuber.

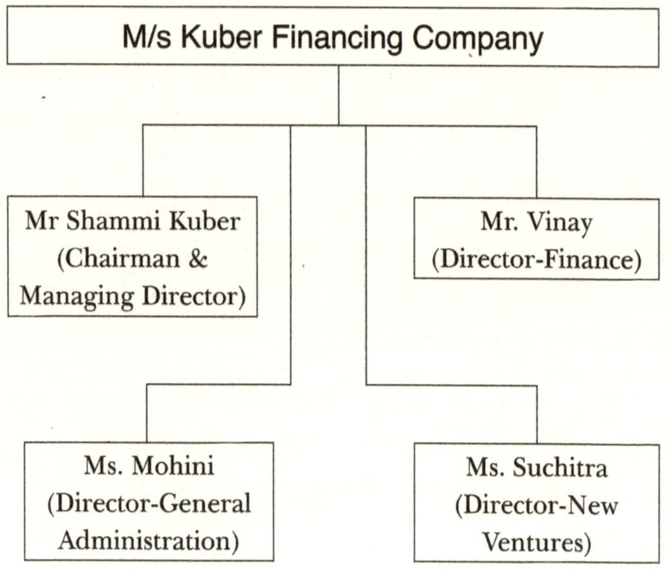

Suchitra was not interested in the family business. She wanted to become a model. She had a big fight with her father regarding this. His father, Mr. Shammi Kuber, doesn't want her daughter to become a model. After all, it was the reputation of his prestigious family. So, the other night, Suchitra escaped from their family bungalow.

Ms. Mohini told Vinay to go in search of Suchitra and bring her back to the family. So Vinay, too, escaped in search of Suchitra. Shammi Kuber was in search of their children, and he was very angry with them that they left the house without his concern.

Suchitra was an ongoing model under the guidance of ***Kamalakh Hazaria.***

*****

After the completion of the Bharatanatyam Class, Sharada and Shikha Thakur (younger daughter of the Thakur Family) came from the class talking to each other. Shikha also helped Sharada financially by learning the classes and knowing her interest in dance.

Sharada and Shikha were good friends in Bharatnatyam Class, and they shared a very good rapport with each other.

They were still in the dance compound; there was one young man hiding behind the tree; he was Kiran Singhal (the Younger son of the Singhal Family). He waved his hand for Sharada.

Shikha asked the whereabouts of the young man. Sharada said she was in love with that young man whose name was Kiran.

Shikha: Okay, Sharada, you carry on.

Sharada: Arey, wait a minute. What about your love, in what state is it, and who is he?

Shikha: He is Ajay Singhal, the elder son of Ajar Singhal from the Singhal family.

Sharada: Then you must meet my lover.

Shikha: why?

Sharada: Because he is Kiran Singhal, the younger son of Ajar Singhal and your lover's younger brother.

Then Shikha met with Kiran and told her entire story with Kiran. Kiran and Sharada promised to join Shikha with Ajay Singhal. Soon, they became good friends, and they were going to become relatives.

CHAPTER 17

Family Gathering at Shabhishak Bungalow

At the Shatbhishak Family Bungalow

All the family members from Shatbhishak, Swarnalekha, and Dhulipala were assembled on their backyard lawn and had a great casual gala time. At that time, Thakur Family members also joined them.

Sanjay Thakur (M/s Thakur Constructions) was a very good friend of Swaminatham (M/s Shatbhishak) and Viswanatham (M/s Dhulipala Textiles). All four family members got busy talking with each other.

Shatbhishak, Shikha and Kishore were on the other side of the lawn having their own petty chat.

Shikha: Brother, what is the progress of my lover Ajay Singhal?

Shatbhishak: My sister, don't worry. I will manage things soon. Ajay, I, and Srikanth are classmates, and it's just a cakewalk for me to get closer to each of you.

Kishore: What? Shikha, you are in love with Ajay Singhal.Wow!! That's good news.

Shatbhishak: Don't worry, Shikha. I had made arrangements for Srikanth and Shirormani to get together, and now I will get you and your lover together. By the way, Kishore, do you need any help in the field of love? You can consult both of us; now we are experts in the field, you know.

While in the talk of older family members:

Sanjay Thakur: Swaminatham, you have given my daughter a huge responsibility.

Swaminatham: Don't worry. Vishwanath's Son Srikanth and my son Shatbhishak are there to support her.

Then, a luxurious car stopped at the portico of the Shatbhishak Bungalow. Srikanth and Shirormani stepped out of the car. All the members stopped talking, and they were looking at the pair of Srikanth and Shirormani, and they all felt that '*both are made for each other.*'

Only Shatbhishak, Kishore, Shikha and Srikanth knew that Srikanth was in love with Shirormani. Shirormani was also not aware of what was going on around her.

*****

The days passed very quickly; Srikanth and Shirormani, Shatbhishak and Rohita, along with Kishore, got very busy with their new company project, 'SWARNABHISHAK'.

Rohita was playing her dual role as Lalitha, but she was not able to go to the Goutampur village frequently.

Shikha was waiting for the chance to meet her lover, Ajay Singhal. Sharada and Kiran were engrossed in love with each other.

In Calbrey Residence, Sunitha was slowly able to improvise her husband Anurag's behaviour.

Manasa and Suchitra were ongoing modelling under the guidance of *Kamalakh Hazaria*.

At Shatbhishak Company

Mayank (Owner of Always Open Garage) was appointed to work with the model designs, and he was reporting to Vinod. Vinay was taking care of accounts in Shatbhishak as a Junior Accounts Officer; no one was aware that he was the son of Shammi Kuber. After analysing his work efficiency in a few months, he was given the hike as the Assistant Manager (Accounts).

At Calbrey Company

Vinod had given the stolen new designs of Shatbhishak to Calbrey, and now Calbrey was working on those models to release in the market ahead of Shatbhishak.

Red Rainbow City was very busy with family business tycoons!!

CHAPTER 18

Shirormani's Heart Beats for Srikanth

Shiroramani was thinking of Srikanth, and she was thinking that she had come very close to Srikanth. The way he talks, the way he expresses himself and the way he gels with her impresses her very much. She felt that her days wouldn't pass without Srikanth.

Srikanth had all the qualities she dreamt of in her future husband or boyfriend. The atmosphere was perfect; the birds were chirping in pairs, the sun was rising, and the cool breeze was blowing.

Srikanth and Shirormani were going towards the goutampur village for a short romantic trip. Srikanth was able to sense the love emotions for him on the face of Shirormani. Even though they haven't proposed to each other that they are in love, their hearts have already exchanged the message of love with each other!!

In true love, the body is not required, but the pure heart is required to feel the love. And where there is true love, there is no scope for unhappiness. Usually, evil comes up when love is misused or used in the wrong manner. Love brings individuals together; they form a small unit called family, and family builds society, and society builds nations, and all nations together build the world!!

Shirormani and Srikanth were now passing from the paddy fields of Goutampur village, where they saw two young lovers talking to each other. When Srikanth paid attention to them, he saw that they were neither else but Shatbhishak and Rohita, but they were dressed in village attire.

Srikanth stopped the car, and both Srikanth and Shirormani went closer to them to meet them. The two lovers were Suryaa and Lalitha (Rohita). Rohita didn't want to be captured about her dual life, so she continued acting as Lalitha in village slang in front of Srikanth and Shirormani.

Srikanth and Shirormani were stunned to note that there are the same set of people with different names. Srikanth even thought that Shatbhishak was acting as Suryaa. When he didn't find a black mole on Suryaa's right jaw, he got to know that Suryaa and Shatabhishak were different people because Shatbhishak had a mole on his right jaw. The black mole was the only difference between Shatbhishak and Suryaa.

At Goutampur Village

In Seth Lampatlal's house, his son Birju packed his baggage to go to his uncle's house (Ratnam-M/s Calbrey Company), who was a distant relative of Lampatlal. Birju got on the bus from the village outskirts and went to Red Rainbow City to meet his uncle Ratnam.

At Red Rainbow City

Calbrey Company launched their new petrol and diesel design models emitting less pollution (stolen from M/s Shatbhishak Company), and because of that, they got hefty orders. The Red Rainbow pollution control Chairman even declared the **"the man of pollution controller award"** to Mr. Ratnam, Chairman and Managing Director of M/s Calbrey Company, for making the new vehicle models that are more eco-friendly and pollution free.

This was a great setback to M/s Shatbhishak Company; they were stunned to note that the same design model they had made in their research laboratory was released ahead of them by their competitor company. The market was taken over by Calbrey Company ahead of Shatbhishak Company.

Now, the Shatbhishak Company has decided to launch the same models with little modifications and at a 25% lower price than the one offered by Calbrey Company.

From this, it was a clear indication for M/s Shatbhishak Company that there was someone in their Company who was leaking their secrets to Calbrey Company. So, the heads were instructed to be more vigilant while manufacturing the designs of vehicles.

Since Shatbhishak Company had declared their new vehicle models emitting less pollution and priced 25% less than Calbrey Company, many people cancelled bookings from Calbrey Company, and they approached Shatbhishak Company to take delivery of the new vehicles. But there were few who struck with the Calbrey Company.

In this manner, the Company's market share was captured almost equally. Making none of them lead the market.

CHAPTER 19

Vinod's Real Identity Is Under Jeopardy

At the Calbrey House

Birju has arrived from Goutampur village, and he brought various goods such as rice bags, wheat bags, sugarcane, jackfruits, etc., from the village. Mr. Ratnam had about 100 acres of land in Goutampur village, which was taken care of by Lampatlal, who was the Village Head in Goutampur Village and also a distant relative of Mr. Ratnam.

All these goods were brought from his cultivated land. Anurag and Sunita received Birju, and other family members also joined them. The Calbrey Bungalow was filled with cereals and fruits.

*****

During these days, ***Mr. Vinay*** (Assistant Manager in Shatbhishak Company) was getting close to ***Ms. Nirmala*** (Assistant Manager of Computer Division in Shatbhishak Company). One night, as they were coming out of Hang Ho Restaurant, they saw Mr. Vinod, who worked in M/s Shatbhishak Company as Head of Designs, entering the bungalow of Mr. Ratnam (Chairman & MD of Calbrey Company) in his car.

They reported this incident to Mr. Srikanth and Mr. Shatbhishak, as well as to Mr. Swaminatham. They all needed solid proof, which Vinay and Nirmala did not have. In this manner, for the time being, Vinod was rescued from being caught. Vinod became more vigilant than before.

Now Vinay told this matter to his friend Mayank, and they both decided to delve deeper into this matter and catch Vinod red-handed.

*****

At Red Rainbow City

Mr. Ratnam, Kalyan, and Birju were travelling together in the car, discussing their crucial business points.

Ratnam: I was expecting the launch of our new model vehicles with less emission would give a big blow to M/s Shatbhishak Company, but they applied good tactics of reducing the prices of their vehicles and launched them in the market. Now we must think of major strategies to grab the market share from Shatbhishak Company.

Kalyan: Don't worry, Dad. We have captured the Windsun Finance Company and are planning to acquire M/s Singhal Polymers. We are equally powerful as M/s Shatbhishak Company. These days, Mr. Pathak (Chairman & MD of M/s Windsun Finance Company) and Mr. Ajar Singhal (Chairman & MD of M/s Singhal Polymers) are under our influence.

Ratnam: But, son, we must weaken the influence of M/s Shatbhishak Company. The Dhulipala Family and Thakur Family are very close to them and support them in all aspects.

Suddenly, Birju saw the photo of Shatbhishak that appeared in the leading magazine of Red Rainbow City, regarding his new company M/s Swarnabhishak Company. He was stunned and said, "Arey, how did the photo of Suryaa end up in the magazine?"

Kalyan saw the photo and said, "Stupid, this is not the photo of Suryaa; this is the photo of Shatbhishak, who is now the Chairman of M/s SWARNABHISHAK Company, which will manufacture solar equipment-fitted vehicles."

Birju: But, Uncle Ratnam, there is one person named Suryaa in our village who looks like Shatbhishak. If we capture him and send him in place of Shatbhishak, you will get all the top-secret information, and you can weaken both companies.

Ratnam: (laughing cruelly) Very good plan, my dear Birju. You go to the village and capture Suryaa, and here we will capture Shatbhishak and Rohita (Daughter of Narayan), and we will make them dance to our tune.

After that, Birju left for Goutampur Village to capture Suryaa, and Ratnam and Kalyan got busy capturing Shatbhishak and Rohita.

CHAPTER 20

M/s Singhal Polymers Captured By M/s Calbrey Company

Srikanth and Shirormani, Rohita and Shatbhishak were called back to Red Rainbow City to take a few crucial decisions in M/s Shatbhishak Company.

*****

At Red Rainbow City: (at Ajar Singhal's Bungalow)

Mr. Ajar Singhal, Aparna Singhal, Ajay, and Kiran were seated silently, thinking about something very seriously.

Ajar Singhal finally broke the silence and said, "Aparna, we are mere stooges in the hands of Mr. Ratnam. I don't know how he got my signature on the blank papers and captured my whole company."

Aparna replied, "Don't worry, we must think of a plan to retrieve those documents from that cruel man."

Ajar continued, "I was in darkness for many days; even Mr. Swaminatham (Chairman of M/s Shatbhishak Company), Srikanth, and Shatbhishak hinted that I should be very cautious when dealing with Mr. Ratnam, as he is a cheat. They advised against any joint venture with him. But I blindly and rashly told them not to interfere in my business matters, and today I am facing the evil consequences."

Ajay consoled him and said, "Dad, don't worry; this is not only your problem but ours as well."

Kiran: "Brother, if you agree, I will confront Mr. Ratnam and send goons on him to teach him a lesson."

Ajar responded, "No, my son, don't engage in any violent activities; it will only make things worse. He is well-connected too."

Ajay: "Then, Dad, there is only one way. I will talk to Srikanth and Shatbhishak. They are my classmates, and I am sure they will help us rescue ourselves from the clutches of Mr. Ratnam."

The problem, Woe, and Dissatisfaction are always with mankind, but at that time, they must be more patient and should not get carried away with evil thoughts. Actually, the problematic period tests one's ability; if he succeeds in that period, he never fails again. If he loses his patience, then for him, life will be just like death every hour, every minute. So, it is always said that: "***Patience and Courage are the two good long-lasting weapons of man.***"

*****

One night, Vinay, Mayank and Nirmala were waiting in the car to catch Vinod red-handedly. In the meantime, they saw Vinod's car moving at a very high speed; they started following the car, but the car was lost in the night.

Vinay and Mayank came out of the car while Nirmala was still seated inside. They looked in all directions, but they could not find a trace of Vinod's car where it had vanished. At that time, suddenly, three jeeps surrounded Mayank and

Vinay. The three jeeps were filled with goons. They slowly got down and attacked Mayank and Vinay and started beating them.

Nirmala immediately called Srikanth and dictated the whole incident to him. In the meantime, a car with powerful headlights stopped before the three jeeps on that lonely street. The rogues suddenly stopped beating them. A dynamic person came out of the car; he was none other than Shatbhishak.

He said: "*Hey guys, why are you fighting with those guys who don't know fighting? Come on, I will teach you guys how to fight.*"

After that, Shatbhishak jumped on them like a tiger and started fighting with them. In the meantime, Srikanth arrived, and he, too, exchanged his blows and kicks with the rogues. Both Shatbhishak and Srikanth captivated the rogues with their strong kicks and blows, which made the rogues run away, leaving their jeeps.

All of them were safe now.

CHAPTER 21

Dharmasena Takes Shatbhishak's Place

On the next day, a meeting was called at the Shatbhishak Company with various department heads and directors of the company.

Mr. Swaminatham propounded: "Dear Ladies and Gentlemen, as we all know, our business secrets are leaking, and our lives are in danger too. Our opponent, Mr. Ratnam, is not doing business now but is playing a different game. For that, he may also use illegal means and power, which may not be good for our company. Hence, I have decided to keep security for our company and for the company heads."

Then he introduced the Chief Security Officer- ***"Mr. Ashish Singh."***

Ashish Singh was the head of the security. He was also secretly assigned to solve the mystery of Vinod, whether he was a legitimate member of the company or an illegitimate member.

*****

Rohita came to her family bungalow, quickly entered her grandfather's room, and started going to Gautumpur Village in a small rail cabin. But the rail cabin was struck up due to technical reasons, so she was forced to come back to the basement of her grandfather's room. Rohita wanted to tell Suryaa about her dual life, and so she was very eager to meet Suryaa.

She decided to go to Goutampur Village in her car and started going alone towards the outskirts of Red Rainbow City. Suddenly, someone came in front of her car, and she applied emergency brakes on her car. She stepped down to see what had happened to that person, but she was captivated by two goons.

*****

At Goutampur Village

Suryaa was waiting for Lalitha near an old palace, which was on the outskirts of the village. There,

Birju arrived with twenty rogues and instructed them to capture Suryaa. Suryaa engaged in a long and intense fight with them, but they eventually overpowered him and took him to Red Rainbow City.

At Red Rainbow City

In Shatbhishak Company and in Shatbhishak Cabin:

Shatbhishak and Shikha were engaged in conversation. In the meantime, Shatbhishak received an intercom call informing him that Ajay was coming to meet him. Shikha's heart raced as she was about to see Ajay and, of course, talk to him.

Ajay entered the cabin, and Shatbhishak greeted him, and he introduced him to Shikha.

Ajay hesitated to talk with Shatbhishak about his father's company being captured by Ratnam by cheating. But Shatbhishak understood that Ajay had come to him to attain his help.

So Shatbhishak said: "Don't worry, Ajay. I will help you get your company back, and for that, I have a plan."

Shatbhishak propounded the plan to Ajay and Shikha. Shatbhishak told Ajay to continue the job of Head of Marketing and Strategies at Calbrey Company and told them to join Shikha as his personal secretary at Calbrey Company.

Shatbhishak continued: Shikha will help you search for top-secret information from the Calbrey Company and will pass it on to you. You can pass the information on to me, and then we will plan to capture those sensitive documents from the Calbrey Company.

Ajay and Shikha were ready for the plan. Shatbhishak said: "I am sending my heartiest sister, Shikha, with you to Calbrey Company. Please take care of her as a bodyguard and safeguard her."

Ajay replied: "Don't worry, Shat, I will safeguard her life more than my life."

Shikha looked at Shatbhishak, thankful for helping her to come near Ajay, who was her lover. Ajay and Shikha left the cabin together.

After they left, Pappu entered the cabin of Shatbhishak, who was appointed there as a peon in the office. He said: "Well, Dharmasena, you are not only a true carbon copy of Shatbhishak's face, but you are another Shatbhishak as well. No one in the office was able to capture you, even your sister Shikha and friend Ajay Singhal."

Dharmasena (who was acting as Shatbhishak) spoke: "Pappu, don't talk loudly or else we will be caught, and the whole plan of Shatbhishak will be spoiled; we must be very grateful to Shatbhishak for helping us."

CHAPTER 22

The Veil of Suryaa and Lalitha is Lifted

At Red Rainbow City

Suryaa was tied, and he was brought into the secret godown of Mr. Ratnam, and he was thrown into a small prison, where Rohita was also present.

Birju told his goons: "Hey guys, take care of both the people and make sure that they don't escape from the prison. I am going to bring my uncle Ratnam."

There is a Prison:

Rohita was shocked to see Suryaa in the prison along with her. She quickly untied Suryaa, hugged him, and kissed him, but she was not able to control her emotions and started crying.

Suryaa consoled her. Rohita took Suryaa away from the prison doors and took him to the lonely prison walls and said the following: "Suryaa, I had been unfaithful to you; I had hidden a big secret with you, and today I am going to tell you the secret."

Then Rohita shared her whole story of how she got into her grandfather's room, read his diary, got to know about the secret rail cabin under his room, and transformed into Lalitha in Goutampur Village and Rohita in Red Rainbow City. She continued and said that she was about to come to Goutampur Village to tell him about this truth, but she was captivated.

Suryaa listened to her story with rapt attention and talked with her: "Rohita, you are not an unfaithful lady because you were always my love, and forever, you will be the love of my life till my last breath."

Suryaa revealed his secret: He is not Suryaa but Shatbhishak (Chairman of M/s Swarnabhishak Company). He also dictated his part of the story; he too wanted to be free from the tension of life, so during his experiments in his secret laboratory on the computer, he was able to develop a programme by which a person can be transferred from one place to another within nanoseconds!!

He also said that the place where the person wants to go has to be set on the map and executed through the programme. Soon, the person will be transferred to that place. So, using this technology, he had acted in dual life in two different places. He acted as "Suryaa" in Goutampur Village and "Shatbhishak" in Red Rainbow City. No one was aware of his experiment except himself.

He said one day, he got an unknown call from an unknown number and was told to come to a haunted house on the outskirts of Red Rainbow City. When he went there, there was one man who tried to hit him on the head with a stick, but he got rescued and found Dharmasena in front of him, who looked like him. Dharmasena wanted to take Shatbhishak's place forcibly, but Shatbhishak passed the hands of friendship towards him and said that he would help him.

After that, he prepared Dharmasena secretly like Shatbhishak and appointed Dharmasena's friend Pappu as a peon in his office. When Shatbhishak was away as Suryaa then Dharmasena used to take the role of Shatbhishak. So, in this manner, they carried out their roles.

Shatbhishak said that he originally had a black mole on his right jaw, but when he was acting as Suryaa, he covered his jaw with artificial skin. Now, that mole was the only difference between Shatbhishak and Dharmasena.

He also said that a small computer was fitted in his watch at present where the vanishing programme is loaded, so they can easily vanish from that prison. But he wanted to know who was behind all these things and who was conspiring against him and his Company. So, at present, he wanted to see them and talk to them as Suryaa so that he could confuse them and captivate them to the police.

Rohita was stunned to hear this from Shatbhishak. She went closer to him and said: "*I like you as Suryaa only. Once all these things get settled, we will settle in Goutampur as Suryaa and Lalitha.*"

Shatbhishak: Very True, Rohita. I, too, feel the same.

CHAPTER 23

Dharmasena is Being Exposed

At Red Rainbow City, in M/s Shatbhishak Company

Mr. Swaminatham, Ms. Vishali, Mr. Suryanatham, Mr. Srikanth, Mr. Shirormani, etc., along with Mr. Ashish Singh, were present. Dharmasena (who was acting in the role of Shatbhishak) entered the conference hall, and Pappu also entered along with him.

When Ashish Singh saw Pappu, he suddenly had doubts about him. Dharmasena didn't want to come before Ashish Singh due to fear of being caught. The fearful and hesitating body language generated doubt in Ashish Singh's mind, and he went near Pappu. Pappu wanted to escape from the conference hall, but Ashish Singh caught hold of him and asked him sternly: "*Hey Pappu, what are you doing in this Company?*"

Everyone was astonished by Ashish Singh's behaviour. Then Mr. Swaminatham asked: "Mr. Ashish, what's the matter? What has happened?"

Ashish Singh: "Sir, he is Pappu, the friend of the robber Dharmasena. I know both of them very well. I wanted to know why and how he had entered this, Company."

All the members in the conference hall were on high alert. Dharmasena was afraid of being caught, and he wanted to rescue Pappu from Ashish Singh's clutches. He entered in between Ashish Singh and Pappu: "What happened? Why are you torturing that poor fellow?"

Ashish Singh looked at Dharmasena and said: "Hey, you are Dharmasena!"

Everyone was shocked, and Mr. Swaminatham spoke in a dynamic voice: "Mr. Ashish Singh, he is my son Shatbhishak and co-owner of this Company. He is not Dharmasena."

Everyone supported Mr. Swaminatham on this point. But Ashish Singh said: "Okay, sir, this fellow may look like your son, but Dharmasena is a great robber, and I can prove it."

Then Ms. Vishali interrupted: "Mr. Ashish Singh, you are crossing your limits. He is my son Shatbhishak, and I can prove it. He has, by birth, a black mole on his right jaw, which is very unique and differentiates him from any other similar-looking person."

Ashish Singh checked the jaw of Dharmasena and found the mole, but when he scrubbed at the mole, it just came off. Actually, it was not the original mole, but it was added to make Dharmasena look like Shatbhishak.

Mr. Swaminatham and Ms. Vishali were shocked; they were not able to understand what was going on in their Company.

Mr. Ashish Singh said: "Dharmasena has a scar on his left hand, which shows that he is not Shatbhishak but Dharmasena. I worked as a jailor before, and this fellow was a prisoner. He tried to escape from the jail, and he used a knife to kill me, but I rescued him, and in turn, his arm was injured by the knife, which made a deep scar on his arm."

Ashish Singh showed the scar to everyone, and everyone present there was stunned that Dharmasena and Shatbhishak were identical, just like twins. Vishali declared that her son doesn't have any scar on his left arm. Then, security guards captured both Dharmasena and Pappu.

Vaishali said: "How is it possible I have only one son and don't have any twin brothers? If he is not Shatbhishak, then where is my son?"

Ashish Singh: "Madam, sometimes it happens that some faces are very much identical, but they are not born twins. For example, we can see Mr. Swaminatham and Mr. Suryanatham. They look like twins, but they are not. You don't worry, Madam; I will reveal the secret of Shatbhishak from Dharmasena in my own way."

Then, Vinod wanted to use this situation to safeguard himself, and he said: "Alas, the culprit who was leaking our company's top-secret information to Calbrey Company has been found."

Ashish Singh said: "Yes, this is quite possible."

Then Srikanth intervened: "But sir, I have seen one more identical face of Shatbhishak in Goutampur village. He was telling me that he was "Suryaa." I also saw a young lady along with him who was identical to Mr. Narayan's daughter Rohita; there, she told me her name was Lalitha.

Everyone was stunned that there were identical people and identical people similar to Shatbhishak and Rohita. Vinod was thinking of a chance to tell all the secrets and incidents to his father Ratnam and use this situation in a way that was favourable to them.

CHAPTER 24

The Real Enemy of M/s Shatbhishak Company is Known

At Ratnam's Godown

Shatbhishak and Rohita were brought out of prison. Birju, Ratnam and Kalyan were standing before them. At that time, Ratnam got a phone call from Vinod; he said there were three identical faces of Shatbhishak- one the original one, He Himself, the second being Dharmasena, and the third one being Suryaa. He also revealed that there are two identical faces of Rohita and Lalitha.

Ratnam got this information and, pulled his hair in confusion, and said to Kalyan and Birju: "*I have heard of duplicate people but never heard of triplicate persons. The person named "Dharmasena" was caught by Ashish Singh; he was acting as Shatbhishak.*

> *Now our plan is we will send this fellow 'Suryaa' as Shatbhishak, and if we find the original Shatbhishak, we will kill him and declare that Suryaa is dead; if Shatbhishak is already dead, then we will kill that Dharmasena and declare him as Suryaa. This fellow will not be caught, and Vinod and this fellow both will work for us, and we will take over the major market share."*

Shatbhishak and Rohita were keenly listening to their conversation and came to the conclusion that "*Vinod*" is the hidden culprit in the M/s Shatbhishak Company. Vinod was acting as a loyal employee, and they also concluded that Dharmasena was caught and must have been rescued.

Since Shatbhishak used to take the role of Suryaa, he used an artificial skin layer to cover his right jaw black mole. Here, he was caught while he was in the role of Suryaa, so his mole was covered by a layer. Ratnam went close to Suryaa (Shatbhishak, who was in the role of Suryaa) and warned them to either work for him or die instantly. Suryaa said he wanted to live rather than die instantly. Ratnam said that he would give a hefty amount in exchange for work done by Suryaa.

Rohita said that she was not Rohita but Lalitha, who had come in the place of Rohita to capture the whole property of Rohita so that she and Suryaa could enjoy it for the rest of their lives. She underwent training to become Rohita and learnt English and the etiquette of rich people for almost three months. She also learnt how to drive a car.

For this, Birju said: "Yes, uncle, it seems she is telling the truth because I haven't seen Lalitha for almost a few months in Goutampur Village. I got the message that she had left the village and had gone for her sister's marriage, as she is telling that she had come in the place of Rohita, she had killed her or vanished her from this world."

Finally, Rohita (who was acting as Lalitha) was sent along with Shatbhishak (who was acting as Suryaa) to act as Rohita. Both of them were given standing orders that if they acted smart, they would be killed instantly, and they must report their every moment to Vinod and should have taken guidance from him. They should act according to Vinod's instructions.

Ratnam sent Birju to Goutampur just in case Suryaa or Lalitha escaped; then, they would reach the village. Suryaa, aka Shatbhishak, and Lalitha, aka Rohita, succeeded in their plan; hence, they had many things to be done after reaching M/s Shatbhishak Company.

*****

Soon after reaching the Company, Suryaa, aka Shatbhishak, and Lalitha, aka Rohita, reported to Vinod as they were told to do so. In the absence of Vinod, Shatbhishak and Rohita met with Swaminatham, Suryanatham, Srikanth, Shirormani and all the key persons of the Company and told them the truth that Suryaa is no one else but Shatbhishak and Lalitha is no one else but Rohitha and both are fine.

Then they dictated the whole story that Dharmasena is a good person, but 'Vinod' is the actual culprit and the son of Mr. Ratnam (Chairman and MD of M/s Calbrey Company), who is involved in stealing the designs from M/s Shatbhishak Company.

Hence, Shatbhishak said that he had a plan and that everyone should act as if they were unaware of Vinod's unfaithfulness, and still, they all consider him a very loyal and faithful employee.

Dharmasena was released from prison, and Vishali got pity on him and felt that he was born and brought up in an uncivilised and unhealthy atmosphere; hence, he might have turned out to be a rogue. She declared that she has two sons from hereafter, "*Shatbhishak*" and "*Dharmasena.*"

Everyone was happy at that time. Now, it was the turn of Shatbhishak Company members to teach the cruel Ratnam a lesson.

*****

Ajay has appointed Shikha as his personal secretary in Mr. Ratnam's Company, and he continued working as Head of Marketing and Strategies. Mr. Pathak (Chairman & MD of Windsun Financing Company) was also helping them as he was also included in the plan.

Shikha investigated that Ratnam had a private room behind his cabin walls, and the wall could slide once the respective lever was operated or pressed. The trigger or remote of the sliding wall was hidden under the small statue, and the statue was fixed on the wall.

Tippan was a cunning person who was working in Mr. Ratnam's office. He was greedy for money, and he was ready to do any type of work for the sake of earning money. Shikha found him and, made friends with him, and tipped him to get the signed Company papers of M/s Singhal Polymers and M/s Windsun Financing Company, in which both declared that their Company's control would be transferred to Mr. Ratnam.

It was a dark night. Ajay, Shikha and Tippan came to Mr. Ratnam's office. Ajay and Shikha sent Tippan to bring the papers of M/s Singhal Polymers and M/s Windsun Financing Company. Ajay and Shikha parked their vehicle on the other side of Mr. Ratnam's office, ready to escape with the secret papers.

Tippan entered the office and was told to stop at the security gates. Then Tippan said he had some leftover work to do in his purchase department, as he was working in M/s Calbrey Company as Assistant Manager (Purchases). However, security guards said that they would confirm this matter with Mr. Ratnam or with Mr. Kalyan, and only after their confirmation will they allow him inside the office.

When Ajay saw that the situation was getting out of control, he entered with a car and said: "Hello, security guards, allow him in the office. I am the Head of Marketing and Strategies, so there is no problem." Security guards were convinced that a senior official was granting

Tippan permission to go inside the office, so they allowed him to do so.

Tippan quickly called Ajay from his mobile and told him to come inside the office. Ajay, too, went inside the office, pretending to complete his pending work. He told Shikha, who was in the car, to be ready to escape once the papers were captured. Shikha was under a lot of stress and was afraid of Ajay being caught, so she called Shatbhishak and told them the entire incident.

Shatbhishak was ready with his vanishing programme and was waiting for Shikha's call if any danger arose there. Shatbhishak, along with Dharmasena, Shirormani, Rohita, and Srikanth, were ready in M/s Shatbhishak company's conference hall. Since Shatbhishak had the complete route map of Ratnam's office, he fed in the programme, and in the next moment, Shatbhishak, Srikanth and Dharmasena were inside Mr. Ratnam's private cabin.

Ajay was surprised to see all three of them in Ratnam's private cabin. Then Ajay pressed the lever, which was under the statue on the wall. Tippan was out of the private cabin to keep an eye on the security guards from coming inside suddenly.

The walls were sliding, but it triggered an alarm simultaneously, and the security guards quickly started coming towards Mr. Ratnam's private cabin. As per the plan, Ajay came out of Mr. Ratnam's cabin, and both Tippan and himself went towards his cabin.

Srikanth, Shatbhishak and Dharmasena were locked inside Mr. Ratnam's private cabin. The security guards came to Mr. Ratnam's executive floor and found that the alarm was coming from Mr. Ratnam's private cabin. Soon, Ajay and Tippan reached there as if they, too, were unaware of this incident. The CCTVs on that floor were deactivated by Tippan beforehand, so there was no recording of the incident recorded.

The security guards quickly called Mr. Ratnam and narrated the incident, as they did not have Mr. Ratnam's private cabin keys. Meanwhile, inside Mr. Ratnam's cabin, Dharmasena went behind the walls and found a huge locker. He was trying to unlock it with his robbery mastermind, and Srikanth and Shatbhishak were stopping the walls from being closed while the alarm was in progress. After a little struggle, Dharmasena was able to open the locker.

After some time, Ratnam and Kalyan reached their office and reached the executive block where Mr. Ratnam's private cabin was. When they opened the private cabin, the cabin was very neat and tidy. He then sent all the security guards outside, and only he and Kalyan were present in that cabin. They then opened their safe and found that all the sensitive documents were present. Then they checked the CCTV footage and found that the last 2 hours' footage was not recorded.

They then checked Ajay's cabin and enquired about Tappan, but they didn't find anything suspicious.

*****

At M/s Shatbhishak Company, Conference hall

Shatbhishak, Dharmasena, and Srikanth appeared back and returned safely to where Rohita and Shirormani were waiting for them. In the meantime, Ajay and Shikha also came there.

Shatbhishak: "Dharmasena was able to remove the safe door, but the important papers of M/s Singhal Polymers and M/s Windsun Financing Company were not present there. So he closed the safe and kept the Cabin neat and tidy and ran the vanishing programme and came back here."

After reaching here, we called Ajay and Shikha to come here.

Srikanth: We were unsuccessful in getting the crucial papers of M/s Singhal Polymers and M/s Windsun Financing Company, but we will find a way to get them.

Then Rohita shared her plan with all of them, and all of them liked it.

At M/s Shatbhishak Company

All the important members of the Company were called for the meeting.

Swaminatham propounded: "Dear gentlemen and ladies, as you know, we have two companies, viz M/s Shatbhishak and M/s Swanabhishak. Now, we are planning to launch another project, and it will be headed by our Chief Designer of Vehicles "Mr. Vinod".

Mr. Vinod is very sincere and hardworking, so our Company is giving him the opportunity to lead this project as the general manager. We have launched vehicles with low pollution emissions, and we are in the process of making solar-fitted equipment vehicles; now, we are planning to use biogas for our upcoming vehicles.

We are launching "PROJECT BIOGAS VEHICLES". Mr. Vinod will be the general manager of this project, and he will select his own team and will design the models and show us within the next six months. In this, he will have the support of Shatbhishak and Rohita.

Vinod was very happy that he was not caught, and in turn, the Company gave him an increment and new project responsibility. Suryaa, aka Shatbhishak, and Lalitha, aka Rohita, were following instructions as per Vinod.

CHAPTER 25

Manasa and Suchitra Were Spotted at a Fashion Show

Nowadays, Vinay (assistant manager of accounts in Shatbhishak Company) and Nirmala (assistant manager of the computer division) in Shatbhishak Company were very close, and they are in love with each other.

Kishore (Younger brother of Srikanth) got an invitation for a 'Women Beauty Contest' in 'Dark Den Emporium'. Mayank, Sharada (Sister of Mayank), Vinay and Nirmala were invited. They all decided to go to Dark Den Emporium to have a gala time there.

The beauty contest started, and various models were walking on the ramp and displaying their various designs of clothes from different brands. In the same beauty contest, Suchitra (younger sister of Vinay and daughter of Shammi Kuber) and Maanasa (sister of Dharmasena) also took part.

When Maanasa came in front of everybody, Mayank saw her for the first time. He felt as if there was someone who could still steal his heart without his concern. The next model was Suchitra; when she came in front of everyone, everyone present there in the hall felt very happy. Few blew whistles, and few shouted in ecstasy. When Vinay saw her, he was stunned to see her, and he felt a little embarrassed. He was not used to seeing her younger sister in that manner before, so it was becoming a hard nut to crack.

He noticed that her frilly frock was not covering even her knees, and the portion below her neck was not properly covered, the whistling and screaming of the audience made him go mad, and he came out of the fashion show. Nirmala spotted Vinay going out of the hall, and she followed him.

Nirmala asked Vinay the reason for his frustration then. Vinay said: "Now you have seen a model; she is no one else but my younger sister who ran away from my family to become a model.

I believe she has succeeded in it. We are both children of Mr. Shammi Kuber, the owner of M/s Kuber Financing Company, which provides 60% of financing to M/s Swanabhishak Company."

Nirmala was shocked when she heard the words from Vinay, and then Vinay narrated to her the whole story of why and how he came to Red Rainbow City. In the Women's Beauty Contest, Suchitra was declared the winner, and all eyes were on her. Maanasa also wished her for winning in the contest.

Kishore was an artist; in his college days, Suchitra liked his paintings. Both were classmates from their secondary education times. Both graduated and post-graduated together in Lakshya City.

After their post-graduation, both got separated. Kishore wanted to tell her that she was his inspiration for paintings, and she was his true love. But time did not permit it. Now, after five years, he was seeing on the ramp as a model. He felt his innocent and bubbly lady luck was lost in the glitters of beauty and fashion.

After the completion of the show, Vinay, Nirmala, and Kishore wanted to meet with Suchitra (Kishore did not know that Vinay was the brother of Suchitra). But they did not get the opportunity to meet her.

*****

After completing the Women's Beauty Contest, Vinay, Nirmala, and Kishore left the club. Mayank was still in search of Manasa, but he didn't find her there. Mayank came out of the club and booked a cab for himself, and as he was about to get into the cab, he saw a girl crying at the corner of the club. Mayank approached her to notice that she was no one else but Manasa, for whom he was searching.

Mayank went near her, consoled her as a true friend, and asked the reason for her sadness. She replied: "I wanted to become a model, and this beauty contest was the biggest opportunity for me. But I couldn't succeed in the contest. Now, I don't have any other opportunity left to become a model. Again, I have to wait for six more months, and I don't have financial support for that."

Mayank consoled her and told her that he would support her and, if possible, send her to her village, where she actually belonged.

CHAPTER 26

Rise of Love and Corporate Love Birds

At Calbrey Company

Mr. Ratnam had received the message that Shatbhishak Company was preparing biogas vehicles which use biogas as their fuel. Immediately, Shatbhishak and Rohita came up with the design of the biogas vehicle design and told him they stole it from the Shatbhishak Company and gave it to Mr. Ratnam at his den.

Mr. Ratnam laughed very cruelly and said: "Both of you work for me in this similar manner, and I will become a very rich man."

He gave a bundle of currency to them for the work they did for him. Shatbhishak and Rohita then left from that place.

Mr. Ratnam and his son Kalyan were in deep discussion:

Ratnam: Preparing a car model with biogas is very dirty work, but its fruits will be very sweet.

Kalyan: Yes, Dad, Shatbhishak Company has decided to do this model in the next three years due to lack of funds. But we will complete the manufacturing in just one year and capture the market.

Ratnam: No, my son, complete this project in just six months. Workday and night, I will keep all our finances in this project so that we can dominate the market with a bang, and we will give checkmate to M/s Shatbhishak Company once and for all.

*****

On the other side of Red Rainbow City, In Lover's Garden. Ajay and Shikha came in the car and went inside the garden to sit under the shade of one tree. They saw many lovers engaged with their lovers under the beautiful tree shade.

Shatbhishak and Rohita were seated under the mango tree; under the neem tree, Srikanth and Shirormani were seated. Under the banyan tree, Kiran and Sharada were seated, and under the Oak tree, Vinay and Nirmala were seated, and they were in their own world of romance.

When they all met with each other, there was a great hollow bellow in the garden. Ajay noted that his younger brother Kiran fell in love with Sharada (Mayank's sister). Vinay also noticed that Sharada was in love with Ajay. Finally, the Corporate Love Birds list was as mentioned below:

SHATBHISHAK		ROHITA
SRIKANTH DHULIPALA		SHIRORMANI THAKUR
KISHORE DHULIPALA		SUCHITRA
AJAY SINGHAL		SHIKHA THAKUR
VINAY KUBER		NIRMALA
KIRAN SINGHAL		SHARADA
MAYANK		MANASA

In these pairs, Mayank love for Manasa was one-sided, and on the other hand, Kishore Dhulipala's love for Suchitra was also one-sided.

*****

At Mayank's House

Manasa was packing her bags to go to her village, Uttamlanka; while talking with Mayank, she said her brother's name was Dharmasena. Mayank stopped her, brought the photo of Dharmasena, and showed her to confirm. Then Mayank called Dharmasena told him that his brother was with him, and took her to meet Dharmasena.

After seeing Manasa, Dharmasena was very happy, and Pappu was also happy. Dharmasena thanked Mayank for what he had done.

CHAPTER 27

Suchitra Lands in the Web of Kamalakh Hazaria

At Red Rainbow City

At Kamalakh Hazaria house:

Suchitra and Kamalakh (he was the person who trained Suchitra for the beauty contest) were seated.

Suchitra: Sir, I don't know why Manasa left me. She wanted to become a model, and she was very hardworking.

Kamlakh: Ah! Don't worry about her. Think of the golden time that you will achieve. You have signed various ad films, TV serials, and you have started getting offers in films. You will be one of the stars in the whole of Red Rainbow City.

Then Kamalakh got a phone call, and he became busy talking on his mobile. At that time, Suchitra received a message that someone with the name Kishore Dhulipala was waiting for her to meet her. She quickly went outside and took Kishore to the guest room. Kishore congratulated her for winning the beauty contest.

Kishore: You are not the same innocent girl I met while studying. I feel I don't know this girl who is in front of me.

Suchitra: We are not college-going young chaps anymore. Now we are grown, and we have to choose our own way.

Kishore: I hope you are happy with what you are doing.

Suchitra: I am happy, Kishore, very, very happy.

In the meantime, Kamalakh Hazaria intervened and sent Suchitra inside the house. He looked at Kishore very cruelly and spoke:

"Listen, Mister, don't try to act smart, and don't ever try to come here again. She is my master key to success, and soon, I am going to marry her. If you come in our way, I will smash you."

Kishore: You are a cruel man, and for the sake of your happiness, you are using Suchitra as a pawn.

Kamlakh: Will you go from here on your own, or shall I call security?

Kishore left with a broken heart from there.

At Mayank's House

Nirmala came to Mayank's house asking about Vinay.

Mayank: You have stolen my friend Vinay's heart. Now he is not even talking to me because he is in his own world. I had seen my love Manasa, but I wanted to tell her my heart's wish. She then told me about her brother, and I was not able to convey my heart's wish.

Then Vinay came from inside and said: "Mayank, you are so selfish. You are thinking only about yourself. What about our sister Sharada? Did you know she fell in love with Kiran Singhal, the younger brother of Ajay Singhal and the younger son of Ajar Singhal? So go quickly and talk to Ajar Singhal about our sister's marriage."

Mayank was stunned to hear this news; he then thought that the Singhal family is a very prestigious family, and he is just an ordinary mechanic now, with the opportunity to work in M/s Swarnabhishak Company in the designs department at a lower cadre.

Nirmala: Vinay, your father Shammi Kuber is in Shatbhishak Company; he knows that you are working in M/s Swarnabhishak Company. He also knows that Suchitra won the beauty contest. I have come here to pick you up for your father.

Mayank was stunned to learn the real status of Vinay. Then Vinay narrated the whole story to Mayank, how he came to Red Rainbow City and that Suchitra was his younger sister, and both are children of Shammi Kuber. Vinay thanked Mayank for all the support he provided. He promised that he will talk to Ajar Singhal for Sharada, and he told him to be confident. He said he will always be his friend, and the wall of riches will never come between their friendship.

Vinay told that Suchitra got trapped in the web of Kamalakh Hazaria and she needs to be rescued. Vinay said that Kishore Dhulipala told him all this, and Kishore also knows who Vinay is.

Mayank assured that he will be with Vinay in bringing back Suchitra from Kamalakh's web. Then Vinay, Nirmala, and Mayank went to meet Shammi Kuber in M/s Swarnabhishak Company.

In Swarnabhishak Company (Special Chamber)

Swaminatham, Shammi Kuber, Srikanth, Shirormani, Vishali, Dharmasena, Shatbhishak, and Rohita were assembled along with Ashish Singh.

Ashish Singh: "Don't worry, Mr. Shammi Kuber, we will search for your daughter."

Then Vinay entered the Special Chamber, along with Mayank and Nirmala. Vinay said: "Suchitra is under the control of that cruel Kamalakh Hazaria; he made her win the beauty contest, and now Suchitra is dancing to his tunes."

Then Kishore (Brother of Srikanth Dhulipala) entered the Special Chamber and added: "And Kamalakh Hazaria has arranged a marriage, which is going to take place in the Devil's Den Garden function hall in just two hours. I have come here to inform you and seek help to stop this marriage and rescue Suchitra from the clutches of the cruel Kamalakh Hazaria."

Shammi Kuber burst into fury: "How dare he marry my younger daughter? I will see his end."

Swaminatham: "Don't worry, Mr. Kuber; we have a big band of warriors. They will all go and stop the marriage. I know the Red Rainbow City Commissioner of Police; he will take care of everything."

Mr. Ashish Singh, along with Srikanth, Shabhishak, Dharmasena, Kishore, and Mayank, were ready to intervene in the Devil's Den Garden.

On the other side, Kamalakh Hazaria came to know the fact that Suchitra is the daughter of the business tycoon Mr. Shammi Kuber. He was now in great tension, and he understood that he could not withstand Mr. Shammi Kuber and the M/s Shabhishak Company family members. His devilish brain started working on whom he could ask for help. He then got the thought that Mr. Ratnam from M/s Calbrey Company was a great competitor against M/s Shatbhishak Company family members.

He recalled a time when he met Mr. Ratnam and Kalyan, who were giving warnings to a few builders regarding a business deal, and at that time, Kamalakh Hazaria was of great help to them. Mr. Ratnam handed over his personal visiting card and told him to ring him up just in case of any help. This was the time to ask for help from him.

Kamalakh Hazaria called Mr. Ratnam and said that he wanted to marry Suchitra, who is the daughter of Mr. Shammi Kuber, and for that, he needed his protection and support. Mr. Ratnam had another cruel plan running in his mind; he told Kamalakh to bring Suchitra to his secret den after the marriage was completed in Devil's Den Garden Function Hall.

Mr. Ratnam sent a huge gang of rogues to stop anyone from entering the Devil's Den Garden Function Hall. Mr. Ratnam was looking for this moment to capture M/s Kuber Financing, keeping his daughter Suchitra as an aide.

At Devil's Den Garden Function Hall:

The marriage had already started in Devil's Den, and Shatbhishak and his friends, along with Shammi Kuber, were just thirty kilometres away from the function hall. In the meantime, four trucks blocked their cars, and a large group of goons got down.

Then Shatbhishak, Dharmasena, Ashish, and Srikanth got down and engaged in a big fight with the goons. Mr. Shammi Kuber was left alone in the car, and a few rogues attacked him, captured him, and started taking him away.

In that situation, Shatbhishak ordered Dharmasena and their twenty guards to help Mr. Shammi Kuber. On the other side, Kishore, Vinay, and Mayank were reaching the Devil's Den Function Hall by another route.

In the Devil's Den Function Hall, Kamalakh Hazaria appointed a large group of rogues or goons with the help of Mr. Ratnam to stop the rival party from entering the garden. All the formalities of the marriage were completed, and Kamalakh Hazaria was about to insert the marriage ring on Suchitra's finger. At that moment, Kishore entered with a motorbike and sped into the Devil's Den Garden Function Hall. He soared through the air with his motorbike, leaving behind the appointed goons, and reached near Kamalakh Hazaria, giving him a powerful kick.

The goons started approaching Kishore, then Mayank and Vinay entered the place, and they engaged in a big fight with the goons. Kishore was behind Kamalakh Hazaria, and he delivered five kicks, two significant blows, and three punches, ultimately settling on the food items meant for the marriage function. Suchitra was not aware of what was happening. Everyone who had assembled there to attend the marriage started running from the function hall after witnessing the brawl.

One goon removed a knife from his pocket and started attacking Kishore. Meanwhile, Ajay and Shikha were passing from the Devil's Den Garden function hall; suddenly, Shikha saw Kiran and Kishore and intimated Ajay. Ajay stopped his car and told Shikha to be seated in the car, and he went inside to help Kishore and Kiran.

The goon was ready to kill Kishore with his knife; at that time, Ajay entered there, and he gave a big kick to the goon to settle on the function hall chairs, and he fell there unconscious. Ajay told Kishore to stop Kamalakh Hazaria from taking Suchitra in his car. Now, analysing this situation, Suchitra came to know that Kamalakh Hazaria was a bad person. Then Kishore followed the car of Kamalakh Hazaria in his motorbike; meanwhile, Suchitra was able to open the car door, and she jumped out from Kamalakh Hazaria's moving car.

Kishore stopped his motorbike and took care of her. At that moment, she observed the love for her in Kishore's eyes. She kissed him compassionately, and then they hugged each other. Kamalakh Hazaria stopped his car, and he saw the huge fleet of brave men coming towards him. They were Shatbhishak, Srikanth, Dharmasena and Ashish Singh. He wanted to go back, but he saw another fleet of brave men approaching him; they were Ajay, Kiran, Mayank and Vinay. Mr. Swamintham reached the spot with high police officials, and they arrested Kamalakh Hazaria.

Mr. Shammi Kuber, Suchitra and others were out of danger!!

Mr. Ratnam was very upset that he was not able to utilise the situation and capture M/s Kuber Financing Company.

CHAPTER 28

Changing Times in Red Rainbow City

Mr. Shammi Kuber felt very angry at Mr. Ratnam after knowing that he was behind all this. But he was happy that his children Vinay and Suchitra were with him. Mr. Kuber thanked Mr. Swaminatham and his family friends for helping him.

On the other hand, Anurag (the second son of Mr. Ratnam) came to know about his father's evil ways and his evil ways of doing business with him. He and his wife, Sunitha, decided to leave the bungalow of his father, Mr. Ratnam, and they started living elsewhere.

Mr. Vinod (Son of Mr. Ratnam and GM of Shatbhishak Company) got very busy preparing the new model of vehicles using biogas as the fuel. He didn't have any access to M/s Shatbhishak

Company and M/s Swarnabhishak Company's sensitive data.

Dharmasena's sister Manasa had a secret love for Mayank, and Mayank loved her, too. Sometimes, they will meet and talk for hours together. Dharmasena was also happy to see both of them together.

Days passed very quickly, and the Corporate Love Birds were very happy with their loved ones. In this segment, Mayank and Manasa, with Kishore and Suchitra, joined.

Now, the Shatbhishak Company and Family, the Dhulipala Family, the Thakur Family, the Singhal Family and the Kuber Family were together, and they decided to teach Mr. Ratnam a good lesson.

*****

Soon, the time proved the result. Mr. Ratnam (Chairman and MD of M/s Calbrey Company) launched his new model of vehicles that uses biogas as its fuel. This was a sudden jerk to the people of Red Rainbow City, but not for M/s Shatbhishak Company and Family!!

The Red Rainbow Pollution Board Chairman was ready with another prize to declare for

Mr. Ratnam for using natural fuels to control pollution. But as the people started to take the delivery of the new model cars, they started to face problems such as getting the very dirty smell of biogas and engine parts being damaged very quickly, and liberated huge amounts of smoke, and the vehicles were not able to cover even five kilometres smoothly.

Mr. Ratnam had blindly trusted the stolen design master copy from M/s Shatbhishak Company and had not conducted enough research on the viability of the vehicles. To launch the new design vehicles with biogas quickly, he took numerous loans from various banks and private financial companies.

The next day, newspapers and media outlets displayed headlines such as "***Gobar Man Ratnam's Gober Invention***," "***The Gobar Man of Red Rainbow***," and "***The Big Cheat of Customers***," among others.

All the customers started returning their cars and demanding their money to be returned. The bank and private finance company also pressured Mr. Ratnam to return their principal amounts with interest.

Mr. Ratnam's huge capital was blocked by the new design of cars, and they were badly disliked by the people. Mr. Ratnam did not know what to do. In one of the press conferences, he said that he would sell away M/s Singhal Company and M/s Windsun Finance Company, which were under his control, to pay off the debts.

But the next day, the newspaper's front page and the media declared that Mr. Ratnam had sold his companies, i.e., M/s Singhal Polymers to Mr. Ajar Singhal and M/s Windsun Finance Company to Mr. Pathak respectively.

It was 8:30 am when Mr. Ratnam was sipping his tea, and when he looked at the front page of the newspapers, his brain was jammed. How could he sell M/s Singhal Polymers to Mr. Ajar Singhal and M/s Windsun Finance Company to Mr. Pathak respectively?

Then Kalyan came to him hurriedly, asking why he had done that.

Mr. Ratnam: No, my son, I haven't sold both companies; the newspapers are just creating rumours. How can I do that when we are running into debt?

Kalyan: I don't know why and how you have done so, but see, Dad, I am not going to share any more debts. I want my share of your property, so you need to give me my part.

Mr. Ratnam was lost from all ends. He did not know what was to be done.

M/s Swarnabhishak Company launched their first phase of vehicles running with solar-fitted equipment which used solar energy. Now the public was very afraid after the scandal of M/s Calbrey Company's flop show of biogas model vehicles. But when the public tested the quality, working, and beauty of the cars, the public was very fascinated and attracted. Soon, the public demanded huge vehicle bookings.

Mr. Ratnam did not know how all these happened. He wanted to give the last blow to M/s Shatbhishak and M/s Swarnabhishak Company, so he called Suryaa (acting as Shatbhishak) and Lalitha (acting as Rohita).

Suryaa, aka, Shatbhishak and Lalitha, aka Rohita, entered Mr. Ratnam's den, where Vinod was also present. Ratnam said: "Suryaa, you might be knowing why I called you?"

Suryaa: Yes, sir, you have completely gone bankrupt, and your company is in full debt.

Ratnam (in an angry tone): Hey, you don't say it like that I am drowning. I knew that, but I will not let M/s Shatbhishak Company rise. If I am not winning, then I will not let M/s

Shatbhishak Company and its subsidiaries win either. You have the last task to do, fix all the bombs in the warehouse, factory, and house of M/s Shatbhishak Company and blow everyone up. If anything happens, I will look after it."

Shatbhishak smiled very gently and spoke: "Mr. Ratnam, what do you think of yourself? Do you believe only you have brains, and no one else does? I have come here to bring an end to my master plan."

"Master Plan... what is that master plan?" Vinod and Mr. Ratnam were stunned.

Shatbhishak revealed his true identity: "I am not Suryaa but Shatbhishak, and she is not Lalitha but Rohita; we both actually lead a dual life. I played the role of Suryaa, and she played the role of Lalitha in "Village." Mr. Ratnam and Vinod's heads were blown away.

Ratnam then ordered his men to shoot Shatbhishak and Rohita.

Then Shatbhishak expounded peacefully: "Don't be in a hurry. I will give you enough time to act, but until then, you will listen to my master plan."

He then said: ***"When Rohita and I were trapped in your den, we had made a master plan that we would act as Suryaa and Lalitha and finally fool you. We learnt about your every action. I even knew that Vinod was the person leaking all the information from our Company. But I didn't interrupt and continued the game. I revealed my family and friends about Vinod's dishonesty, and they acted as if they were not aware of Vinod's mischief.***

My father, Mr. Swaminatham, made Vinod the General Manager of the New Project only to keep him busy and disconnected from our Company, so his crucial decisions wouldn't leak. Meanwhile, our company had a secret meeting about the vehicles running on solar energy, and we secretly designed and released them without your knowledge.

The design of the Biogas vehicles, which I presented to you as Suryaa, was not a good design but a faulty one. Those cars couldn't even travel for five kilometres, and the smell of gobar gas was a never-ending problem. You didn't spend a single penny to check whether the design was viable or not, blindly believing in the model and taking huge debts from all the companies."

Meanwhile, through Ajay, I appointed Shikha as your personal secretary. She was able to know about your secret things and took your signature on blank papers without your knowledge, and we moulded them as per our use. We made you sell M/s Singhal Company to Mr. Singhal and M/s Windsun Finance Company to Mr. Pathak. Your original paper in which you have taken Mr. Singhal and Mr. Pathak selling their companies to you is also with us."

Mr. Ratnam and Vinod's minds were jammed, and they could not understand what to do or say.

Finally, Mr. Ratnam gathered himself and said: "Well, great, you are the cleverest business tycoon I have ever met in my life. But you have forgotten that you are in my den, and I will use you and Rohita to get your Company papers in exchange for your life."

Shatbhishak smiled and said: "Mr. Ratnam, I thought you were at least a little bit clever, but you proved me wrong. What do you think? Can you trap me? I had a device to rescue, but before that, you look around."

Ratnam and Vinod looked around to find Dharmasena, Ashish, Srikanth, Vinay, Mayank, Ajay and Police Commissioner Mr. Jaswanth

Rathod entering the den. Soon, police captured Mr. Ratnam and his son Vinod on conspiracy grounds and seized his hideout places and den.

CHAPTER 29

The Marriage of Corporate Love Birds

On the same day, Mr. Swaminatham declared a huge open invitation to all to join in the marriage of seven loving pairs happening at once.

Seven loving pairs getting married at once was a thing of surprise in the business circles and in the business families. All the big personalities were invited to this marriage. The marriage was being conducted in the "Greenland Palace".

The Greenland Palace was decorated with various huge series of bulbs and flowers, and the hoardings of Married Couples were displayed everywhere. From the distance, the palace looked like a rising sun.

There was a huge gathering of reputed persons in the palace; many sophisticated cars were parked around the palace. A special path was decorated for the loving pairs to come on that way. Mr. Swaminatham and Ms. Vishali were busy with their great personalities. Dharmasena, Pappu and Suryanatham were at the entrance of the huge palace gate to invite the guests.

Vishwanath Dhulipala and Parvathi Dhulipala were giving suggestions to the wedding planner for stage decorations. Inside the palace, Mr. Pathak and his two daughters, Sunitha and Pinky, were standing along with their husbands, Anurag and Kalyan.

Ajar Singhal and Aparna Singhal had arrived along with Mr. Shammi Kuber and Mohini, and they immediately met with Mr. Swaminatham and Vishali.

In the meantime, a luxurious car arrived, and Sanjay Thakur and his wife, Ms. Rukmani Thakur, stepped down; behind in another car, Mr. Narayan and his wife, Ms. Parvathi, stepped down. Vishwanath Dhulipala and Ms. Parvathi Dhulipala received them, and they all started going inside the palace together.

Everyone was waiting for the seven cars of the wedding pairs to arrive. Each pair comes in a luxurious car manufactured by M/s Shatbhishak and M/s Swarnabhishak Company. Everybody assembled at the entrance of the Greenland Palace, and then the first car arrived. The first loving pair, Shatbhishak and Rohita, stepped down. Special security guards escorted them to the huge stage, which was decorated with 1000 types of different colours, and sixteen priests were already seated there spelling precious godly hymns.

In the following car, Srikanth Dhulipala and Shirormani Thakur arrived. In the next car, Kishore Dhulipala and Suchitra Kuber arrived. Similarly, in a similar fashion, four other cars arrived, carrying:

Kiran Singhal and Sharada

Ajay Singhal and Shikha Thakur

Vinay Kuber and Nirmala

Mayank and Manasa

They all were surrounded on the big holy stage, and all the seven pairs were seated on the holy stage. This marriage was being telecasted live in all major cities, namely Baharein, Lakshya, Vimalak, and Red Rainbow.

The parents were happy that their children were getting married.

- **Mr. Shatbhishak** (Son of Mr. Swamintham and Ms. Vishali - M/s Shatbhisak Company) was getting married to **Ms. Rohita** (Daughter of Mr. Narayan and Ms. Parvathi - M/s Shatbhishak Company).

- **Mr. Srikanth Dhulipala** (Elder Son of Mr. Vishwanth Dhulipala and Ms. Parvathi Dhulipala - M/s Dhulipala Textiles) was getting married to **Ms. Shirormani Thakur** (Elder Daughter of Mr. Sanjay Thakur and Ms. Rukmani Thakur - M/s Thakur Constructions).

- **Mr. Kishore Dhulipala** (Younger Son of Mr. Vishwanth Dhulipala and Ms. Parvathi Dhulipala - M/s Dhulipala Textiles) was getting married to **Ms. Suchitra Kuber** (Daughter of Mr. Shammi Kuber and Ms. Mohini Kuber - M/s Kuber Financing Company).

- **Mr. Ajar Singhal** (Elder son of Mr. Ajar Singhal and Ms. Aparna Singhal - M/s Singhal Polymers) was getting married to **Ms. Shikha Thakur** (Younger Daughter of Mr. Sanjay Thakur and Ms. Rukmani Thakur - M/s Thakur Constructions).

- **Mr. Kiran Singhal** (Younger son of Mr. Ajar Singhal and Ms. Aparna Singhal - M/s Singhal Polymers) was getting married to **Ms. Sharada** (the only Sister of Mayank - Owner of Always open workshop, which was now an integral part of M/s Swanabhishak Company).

- **Mr. Vinay Kuber** (Elder Son of Mr. Shammi Kuber and Ms. Mohini Kuber - M/s Kuber Financing Company) was getting married to **Ms. Nirmala** (a distant relative of Mr. Swaminatham and Ms. Vishali).

- **Mr. Mayank** (Owner of Always open workshop, which was now an integral part of M/s Swanabhishak Company) was getting married to **Ms. Manasa** (Sister of Dharmasena, who was declared as the Chief Security Officer for M/s Swarnabhishak Company).

During the marriage, everybody came to know about the hidden relationship of **Mr. Ashish Singh** (presently the Chief Security Officer at M/s Shatbhishak Company), who was actually the son of Sanjay Thakur's sister. Mr. Sanjay Thakur was the uncle of Mr. Ashish Singh.

Mr. Pathak's sister had a daughter by the name of **"Sugandha."** Mr. Pathak (Chairman and MD of Windsun Finance Company) approached Mr. Sanjay Thakur (Chairman and MD of M/s Thakur Constructions) for the marriage of Mr. Ashish Singh with Ms. Sugandha, which Sanjay Thakur accepted gleefully.

Finally, the eight pairs' wedding (including Mr. Ashish Singh and Ms. Sugandha) was completed in a grand manner. Many eminent personalities of Red Rainbow and other cities attended this wedding and offered precious gifts to the wedded couples.

*****

After a few days, as decided, Shatbhishak and Rohita settled in the village of Goutampur as Suryaa and Lalitha in Lalitha's grandfather's house. They established a family trust for the welfare of the Goutampur village people and nearby villages.

THE END

Special Bibliography

Prana Healing is a No touch, No drug Prana Therapy.

Prana Violet Healing (PVH) teaches us how to consciously increase the quantity of Prana in our body and how to use it to heal our health problems.

The sun, the planet Earth and other stars and planets, the trees, the seas, the mountains around us – we all share our origin with one Creator, and we all are family members in this universe with a profound invisible connection amongst us. Our thoughts and emotions will instantly connect us to our cosmic counterparts.

The founder of this organisation is **Mr. Sivavikkraman Palani**

For healing and to know more about PVH, kindly log on to:

www.pranaviolethealing.com

The **PSSMovement (P.S.S.M)** consists of many independently functioning Pyramid Spiritual Societies, established in many villages, towns, and cities in different states of India and across the globe.

Pyramid Spiritual Societies Movement is a non-religious, non-cult, non-profit voluntary organisation whose sole mission is to spread "**Anapanasati Meditation**", "**Vegetarianism**", "**Spiritual Science**", and "**beneficial uses of Pyramid Energy**" to one and all.

The founder of this organisation is **Brahmarshi Pitamaha Dr. Patriji Maheshwara Maha Pyramid, located on the outskirts of Hyderabad City in Telangana State of India, is the biggest Meditative Pyramid in the world (the above picture)**

For more details, please visit:

www.pssmovement.org

www.pmconlivetv.com

"MEDITATION MEANS OBSERVATION OF OUR OWN BREATH."

Other Titles By The Author - SID

- *Mr Three Maniac's – Crime Thriller*

www.ingramcontent.com/pod-product-compliance
Lightning Source LLC
LaVergne TN
LVHW091045150826
845673LV00002B/474

* 9 7 9 8 8 9 2 7 7 2 4 6 4 *